HERITAGE RESTORED

Caroline's Heritage Series

Book One:

HERITAGE RESTORED

Gaile Thulson

 Cup of Water Publishing

You have given me the heritage
of those who fear your name.

Psalm 61:5

HERITAGE RESTORED

❧ CHAPTER ONE ❧

Caroline finally stood before the beveled glass front door, fumbling with unfamiliar keys in her growing excitement. Did *any* of this seem familiar? She couldn't be sure. It had been a long journey back to rediscover what she could of a few vague childhood memories. She was afraid to step inside, afraid she would only be disappointed.

"I know I've been here before. My grandparents did live here. I didn't make this up, and they wanted me to have it!" she assured herself, swinging the door open enough to slip inside.

Yes, she did remember! She did have some recollection of the front entry at least. What she could see of the house from where she stood, looked immense measured by her limited life experiences, but it felt like coming home. The house was not as castle-sized as it had seemed to her toddler self; but the oval pattern in the marble floor was still large and grand, though dusty. Her nineteen-year-old self marveled that it belonged to her. She was determined to know, to experience, to *live* this house. There was no one left to object, except the lawyers. Let them think she was visiting before putting it on the market. She was nineteen and alone, but before all the years of internal aloneness, she had known a different kind of existence.

She thought of her mother, her father, her grandmother and grandfather. She remembered being loved. She remembered this house, so she reached for the light switch, rejecting the thought that she might be even lonelier here. Somewhere, somehow, in spite of the hardness and bitterness, in spite of the hurt and pain, there was inside of her a knowledge that life could be different, that it *should* be different.

She had flown in with her backpack, two beat-up suitcases, and three boxes yet to come in the mail comprising all of her worldly possessions. It was late in the day, but she had food in her backpack for at least supper and breakfast. Thin and petite with an athletic build and a small appetite, she rarely finished a restaurant or fast food meal. Paying for one meal usually provided her with enough food for the next meal or two as well. Life and self-reliance had taught her to plan ahead, and she knew that she had enough to get by for now. In addition to making two or three meals out of one, she had learned many ways of economizing during her growing up years, and she would need to keep it up to accomplish her goals. There would be no one to help.

The stillness of the house crept into her consciousness and she took a deep breath with what she realized was relief that she felt no fear and, indeed, did not feel like an intruder. The emptiness of the house was not welcoming, but neither was it frightening. There was peace here, impersonal peace it seemed. She claimed it for herself.

Caroline turned toward the dining room so that she would not have to address the gloominess at the top of the grand, sweeping staircase. She would hurry through the main floor so that she could gather enough courage to explore the upstairs before dark. One thing she could not do was to go to sleep in a strange house without assuring herself it was as empty as she felt it to be.

It wasn't empty of furniture. Passing through the open archway to the left, she stopped, startled by a magnificent rug and the gleam of exquisite old china, silver, and wood. Did people really live like this? All of these beautiful things now belonged to her! Caroline had learned to live frugally long ago, and where she didn't find beauty, she created her own. Her clothing was tasteful though inexpensive, much of it her own design or made-over discount bargains. She knew how to sew and had a knack for dressing becomingly. Careful shopping with a good eye for color, style, and fabric, combined with the ability to see what something could become with careful alteration, had blossomed through necessity into a confidence that she was attractively dressed as the young professional she would someday become. She did not view being poor as a disadvantage. In fact, she supposed it had distinct advantages, as she had developed many skills out of necessity.

Passing carefully through the room, her fingers lingered on the smooth surfaces. She suppressed the immediate desire to dust and polish and forced herself to keep moving. A swinging door led to the butler's pantry, an indulgence to savor later. She could hardly wait to discover her grandmother's treasures, but first things first. The old-world kitchen was spacious, filled with charming accents, and thoughtfully laid out. A cord hung conspicuously over the top of the refrigerator and dangled into the yawning door. Her first job tomorrow would be wiping it out and plugging it in before she made a trip to the nearest grocery store. The refrigerator looked fairly up to date and was in good shape, much bigger and grander than she needed, but fairly energy efficient. Surveying the other features of the room, she doubted that she had ever seen this kitchen's equal in her life. Surely her grandmother had loved cooking here, but then again, she knew little about her grandmother. Perhaps she'd always had help and had never stepped a foot into her own kitchen.

"Well, I can't wait to use it!" she exclaimed appreciatively.

Caroline looked quickly under the sink and into the pantry and broom closets. They were sparsely stocked, but enough canned foods and cleaning supplies remained so that she wouldn't have to start with absolutely nothing. Her spirits lifted. This was possible.

After opening numerous closets and cabinet doors, her housekeeping need-to-know was satisfied for the time being. From the kitchen, she stepped into a corner breakfast room surrounded by windows and appointed with white wicker. It would be lovely in the morning. Storing away another delightful experience for her future, she quickly turned back to explore the rest of the house. Leading to the back door, a small mud room with a utility sink looked perfect for flowers, crafts, and cleaning up from yard work. Cupboards were stocked with vases and flower-arranging paraphernalia. A flower arranging room! It seemed to Caroline a leftover from some bygone era, some outdated novel with a happy ending in which the woman of the house had leisure to wander through her flower garden choosing the perfect blooms to arrange and display in her shining, hospitable house. Caroline closed the door in anger, anger which instantly dissipated with the stunning thought that this was *her* house. *She* would have flower gardens and perhaps a vegetable garden! Would she have time to plant gardens next spring? She had studied online photos of the house and yard nearly every day for the past year, and she knew there were several flowerbeds and a large garden area. It was getting too dark outside to see them, and she had no desire to open the drapes or raise shades that would expose her to the neighbors' views. But tomorrow! Never had she thought with such joy and anticipation about tomorrow! A sudden memory of planting seeds in rows with her mother washed over her, leaving her anguished and yearning. Was it here, in this yard that they had so carefully, so happily placed seeds and covered them with sun-warmed soil?

She walked quickly through the study and bathroom at the back of the house, obviously her grandfather's lair though he had died years before her grandmother, and then she returned to the hallway to brace a kitchen chair under the doorknob to the basement stair. She wanted to feel safe enough to sleep soundly, and the basement could wait until tomorrow. Whatever else was down there, she was quite confident it contained new, high-efficiency furnaces, air conditioners, and hot water heaters. The lawyers had made certain that potential new owners would not be daunted by things needing to be fixed or updated. But right now she needed to finish the job of knowing what was here for her, before darkness came.

Retracing her way to the front, she discovered a beautifully decorated powder room tucked under the stairway and marveled at its perfection. A glance in every direction around the tiny room revealed luxury with no expense spared. Sighing, she turned back across the marble floor, and then exclaimed aloud at the set of wood doors opposite the front entry. In the gloaming, she had not noticed the richly grained cherry and detailed carving. Pushing these tall pocket doors aside, she discovered that they led to a large family room stretching across the central back portion of the house It was comfortably furnished with a thick oriental rug centered between sofas that bookended a massive stone fireplace to her left. A peek behind expansive but informal draperies revealed double sets of French doors opening onto a stone patio along the back of the house. From the family room she turned to the right and proceeded through elegant French doors into the library, a room extending from front to back along the opposite end of the house from the kitchen. She immediately fell in love with the library, full of gleaming wood, a carved limestone fireplace, and books of all kinds protected from dust by shining glass doors. In the front corner of the room, stood a grand piano, framed by windows to the north and east. She looked forward to spending as much time as possible in this room!

Through more French doors into a formal sitting or living room on the front of the house, then circling back through an open archway into the front entry brought her again to the foot of the staircase. She marched up quickly, finding the light switch in the upstairs hall. For one night, lights would blaze through the entire house. This was not the time for economizing on utility bills. It was chilly downstairs, but perhaps she wouldn't need to turn up the furnace yet. It did feel a few degrees warmer upstairs. Utility bills, taxes, and other unavoidables loomed frighteningly large in her budget. With tuition and other college expenses, she dared not ask too many other things of the limited money that remained from what her grandparents had left her.

She explored the master bedroom, closets, and bath, but felt increasingly uncomfortable about moving into what had obviously been her grandparents' tasteful suite. There was another spacious bedroom on the front of the house, and though furnished in neutral colors and style, it seemed feminine in many ways. Was this the room in which her mother had lived her childhood years? She didn't know.

Moving with curiosity through the other rooms, she discovered one that had most likely been Uncle Brad's. Like her mother, he had been so young when he died. How could all of these people be gone? How could an entire family be taken from this earth? What kind of God did things like that? What would her life have been if they were all alive, all here with her now, filling the house with movement and life? Somehow, she hadn't thought of all these empty bedrooms suddenly making the house too large and lonely for one young woman yet to turn twenty. She hadn't thought either, that she would be asking these questions that had no answers. Caroline began to weep. She was surprised to hear the sounds of grief and desolation that were coming from somewhere beyond her control, deep within herself. She made the sounds stop coming from her mouth, crying silently as she descended the stairs for her backpack and suitcases. The front bedroom would be fine for her. She felt sure it had been her mother's. She would think about the other rooms and what they all meant some other time.

Suddenly exhausted, she busied herself with stripping the bed and putting on the clean sheets she had brought with her. The house was dusty, as she had guessed it would be. How could she possibly wash all the bedding and maintain these rooms? She would have to close up the other bedrooms for now. A picture of all in shreds, the house going to rack and ruin like old Miss Havisham's in *Great Expectations*, filled Caroline's mind. Perhaps she was being foolish. Sell such a house, rent it, close up most of it and live in two rooms, all advice she had been given, but the lawyers hadn't known it to be so beautiful nor so full of promise. They certainly knew nothing of her need to make her memories real. Yet how could a nineteen-year-old girl live alone in a house like this and put herself through years of college and graduate school? Not so many years, she reminded herself. She'd already accumulated more than a year's worth of credits and, as for the money, she had done the planning herself. She knew it was financially possible if she were careful, but what if there were things she didn't know?

"No more scaring yourself, Miss Caroline," she asserted out loud. "Sufficient unto the day."

What did that mean? Was it from the Bible, or Shakespeare, or somewhere else? Yes, there were unknowns in the picture, but she would deal with them as they came along. She was young and smart and strong. She did not need a car, she did not need a lot of things, and she did not need anyone else. She had a chance to make it now.

She found blankets in plastic bags on the closet shelves and, knowing that she would be warm and comfortable, prepared for bed. It didn't take long to turn off all of the lights and retreat to her room, locking the door. Her own room. Her own bed. Her mother's room. Her mother's bed? She slept the sleep of exhaustion, like any healthy young body caught up in the ambiguities of life. But now there was hope.

ভাে

Caroline woke later than usual, sunshine already bright behind the window shades. Yesterday had been a long day. She had flown halfway across the country, and she knew from experience that her internal clock would need a week or so to fully adjust to the time change. She seldom needed an alarm clock. Somehow she had always found things to look forward to each day to make morning a wonderful time of day just for her. She had always loved waking up in the morning, and when the sun shone, it had always been easier to think of reasons to be hopeful. But this morning! This morning she lived in a make-believe world. This morning she was truly on her own, on her own schedule with no one demanding her participation, with no one but herself to take care of, with no one's concerns but her own to be met. Her own house! Home! How quickly it became a tentative thought. Home. What did it mean to make this house her home? Whatever it meant, she was going to find out and make it happen.

She stretched and stayed in bed for a few more luxurious thoughts. Being alone was a wonder. A series of foster homes following her parents' deaths had meant she was always alone on the inside but was never allowed to be alone on the outside. Sharing rooms with children who didn't want another "sister," obligations to pitch in and do double duty to earn a place in a family that would never be hers, looking after younger children, and for the last three years tending a terminally ill adult, made this quiet moment one of the more incredible experiences of Caroline's life. She was free! She was of age and she had come fully into her inheritance, an inheritance that she had not even known existed. Why had her grandparents allowed her to live in foster homes, never even sending her a birthday card, and then left their home to her? It may have eventually, automatically passed to her as last of kin, but it hadn't come to her that way. It had been left to her and her alone in her grandmother's will. Perhaps she would find answers here, in this house.

No doubt about it, life was beginning for Caroline now. Her life had been a series of holding patterns like a plane stalled above the runway, waiting to land. But now she had landed. She jumped eagerly out of bed, making it trim and neat before she did anything else. Her normal stretching routine felt great. Time to get busy! She had her very own bathroom, even if this wasn't the master bedroom, and though the bedroom was furnished in neutral colors, the bathroom was pink. Dated, but it suited her. She cleaned it quickly and efficiently. Certainly no one had been using the house since the first cleaning in preparation for listing it with a realtor, but something about this new life made her long for cleanliness and order. She had the name of her grandmother's friend who had arranged for the cleaning crew: perhaps once in a while she could splurge and have them clean the house from top to bottom.

It didn't seem real that she was putting her things away in a place where they would stay, a place that belonged to her, a place where she belonged! The closet was nearly full, but she hung the things she had brought in a small space. There was one empty bureau drawer which she filled, glad that she didn't have to disturb anything to move in. Later she would go through every closet and drawer, every scrap of paper, to discover her heritage, if she had any.

Downstairs, she headed straight for the kitchen: breakfast was her favorite meal. She didn't have milk and cereal, or eggs, but quickly fixed a cup of tea and some instant oatmeal, and then sliced an orange she had brought with her yesterday. Not a bad breakfast, and it would have to do.

After arranging it all on a pretty tray, she eagerly pushed her way through the swinging door to the breakfast room. Dust on the glass tabletop forced her to return to the kitchen for glass cleaner and paper towels, but soon she had the top of the white wicker table sparkling. Now to let in the sunshine! The east windows on the front of the house looked out onto the shady, broad front porch running the entire length of the house; but the windows on the south end of the house were gloriously full of sunshine and color, a result of the view of the side yard with its fall flowers in bloom. To think that every morning she would have breakfast in this lovely room! She paused to breathe in the light-filled air with a sigh of contentment, looking around the room with curiosity. Judging from the attention to detail and the muted blending of pastels in the color scheme, her grandmother must have enjoyed this room. She had made a tasteful, serene setting that anyone would love. A few oversized, strategically placed floral watercolors were attractively framed and tied the room together with peaceful hues. Caroline sighed again with contentment. Perhaps beginning the day like this would help her to cope with the anxieties of trying to hold onto her inheritance.

"Thank you, Grandmother," she murmured hesitantly, but gratefully.

On a side table nearby, was a short stack of books and papers. She liked to read, and eating alone did allow her the luxury of reading at the table. She brought the books to her place and began looking through them. What had her grandmother read at breakfast? One book was a Bible, another a book of poems, and the last seemed to be some kind of guide to readings in the Bible. Some of the kids Caroline admired during high school had talked about the Bible, but she had never really had the chance to look one over. She'd read most of the other books on the school library shelves, but she'd always felt too self-conscious to take a Bible off the shelf. Was this one her grandmother's? Yes, there was her name in the front: Emily Hampden. Well, how did one read the Bible? Start at the beginning and read to the end? It seemed a little intimidating. Could she find one of the readings that the guidebook discussed? She opened to a daily reading and looked at the verses listed: John 14:1-4. A look in the front of the Bible revealed that it contained several varieties of John. Maybe this was harder than it looked. But only one of them was simply "John." Yes, she could find John 14. She turned pages and began to read with astonishment.

Do not let your hearts be troubled. Trust in God; trust also in me. In my Father's house are many rooms; if it were not so, I would have told you. I am going there to prepare a place for you. And if I go

Caroline quickly glanced back at the context, then ahead, and decided it was Jesus talking. God had a house with many rooms just like this one? Was she someday expected to go there? She didn't know the way. Were her parents and grandparents there? She hoped so. Was Mr. Axel whom she had helped care for these past three years there now? She didn't think so. He had not wanted anything to do with God.

Had God perhaps prepared even this house, her grandparents' house, for her? She supposed he had, if there really was a God, if this reading from the Bible were actually true. Perhaps it wasn't just some strange good fortune out of the blue that had brought her to this house. But why would God care so much about her, to give her such a home? She read the passage again while she ate, turning it over in her mind as she returned to the kitchen. Was heaven a real place?

She began wiping out the refrigerator, her mind so full of churning questions that she was finished before she knew it. Plugging in the fridge, she briefly listened to its purr before returning to the breakfast room and the open Bible. "Do not let your hearts be troubled. Trust in God; trust also in me."

"Well, God," she flung aloud to the walls, "if you exist, you're going to have to show me, and not in some mystical, unreal way. You're going to have to show me some way that's real, through people, people who care, because I don't have anyone who cares about me. You took every one of those people away. Why would you do that?"

She brushed aside an angry tear, determined to make her grocery list. What did she really need to get through the next few days? While she was pondering the least expensive solutions to her needs, she sent an email to the law firm. Later today she would make use of her grandfather's out-of-date computer to write a letter formally ending her relationship with the firm. Now that the estate was settled without a doubt, all the necessary things having been done to the house, she was staying. There was no longer a need for the lawyers, and she would not be contacting a realtor. They had expected her to choose a few keepsakes for herself before holding an estate sale. There was not going to be a sale.

Why not have that cleaning crew in to celebrate? Since she had delayed the sale of the house for several months while she had figured out what she was going to do, the house really needed it. She paged through the large file she had accumulated on the house, looking for the name and phone number of the woman the lawyers had contacted. It seemed to Caroline that she had perhaps heard it mentioned that this woman had known her grandmother.

"Mrs. Larson? This is Caroline Engbert, Emily Hampden's granddaughter."

"Caroline? Emily's granddaughter?"

"Yes. I'm not going to be selling the house. I've come to live here, and I wondered if you might arrange for the cleaning crew to come back now that the remodeling and repairs have been done? I'd… I'd like to have the house cleaned again, from top to bottom."

"You're going to be staying? *Oh my dear Caroline*, Emily would be so pleased. To think of all those years she prayed for you! And now you've come home! She must be so happy!"

"You know my grandmother passed away a year ago and left me the house…"

"Yes, yes of course. You must be thinking I'm senile! But I'm sure she and your grandfather are looking down from heaven and know all about it. They wanted so much to give you a home and finally their prayers have been answered. To think of all those years she prayed for you."

"Oh. I… I like the house very much. Were you the one who arranged to have it cleaned before?"

"Yes, I'll have to call them. It's a cleaning company someone in our church has. It may take a few days to schedule. I'm sure they have regular cleaning schedules, but I'll have them call you."

"Could you just go ahead and set it up for any day? I'll call you back tomorrow."

"Well, I guess I could do that. What day would you like them to come?"

"Any day in the next two weeks would be fine, but the sooner the better, because I'll be starting classes in two weeks and then I won't have time to be here when they come."

"Well, I'll see what I can do. If you want the whole house cleaned, I suppose it will have to be a special crew. I'll see what they say. So, you'll call me tomorrow?"

"Yes, I will. Thank you. I'll talk with you tomorrow. Goodbye."

"Goodbye, Caroline. Your grandmother was a wonderful person. I'm looking forward to meeting you!"

"Thank you. Goodbye."

Caroline didn't necessarily want to meet Mrs. Larson, but her friendliness, along with her high opinion of her grandmother, was the cause of an unfamiliar feeling of warmth that confused Caroline. Her grandparents had wanted to give her a home? Then why hadn't they? What did Mrs. Larson mean that her grandmother had prayed for her all those years? Then why had she stayed away? A small chunk of hurt was replaced by confusion and wonder.

Grabbing her empty backpack, she quickly locked the door behind her and hurried down the walk, checking an online map to make sure she knew which way to head to the natural grocery store she'd found in the area. Graceful homes similar to her grandparents' but each a unique design, were scattered around the wide cul-de-sac. Broad sweeps of open lawn with clusters of trees separated the houses, and Caroline hardly noticed the elderly lady, her closest neighbor, working in a flower bed of the adjacent front yard, who looked up with a welcoming smile as Caroline approached.

"Hello!"

"Oh, hello!" Caroline replied.

"I didn't realize they had sold the house." She stood up and removed her gardening gloves. "I'm Martha Lockwood."

"I'm Caroline, the Hampdens' granddaughter. I'm not selling the house after all. I'll be staying."

"Oh! How wonderful to meet you, Caroline! Your grandmother would be so happy to know you're here. She was a wonderful friend and neighbor, and we all loved her dearly. Why, how can we help you get settled? What can we do for you? She would be so happy to know you and your family… are here to stay?"

"Well, I… it's just me, but I really don't need anything. I just need a few groceries. I know it isn't far to the store."

"Let's see, it's about six blocks. I used to walk it more often in my younger days. I'll be going over in my car later. Could I take you?"

"Oh, no. No thanks. I just need a few things. This way, isn't it?"

"Down two blocks," she said pointing, "and over four."

"Thanks! Thanks, ever so much!"

Caroline was off before Martha had a chance to issue the invitation to supper that was on the tip of her tongue. Martha watched Caroline's young, energetic pace take her quickly away.

"Would you like to come to supper?" Martha had to raise her voice to catch Caroline's attention.

"Sometime! Thanks!" Caroline waved as she passed out of polite yelling distance.

So, her grandmother had been a dear friend and a good neighbor of this gracious lady. She felt strangely relieved at this confirmation that her grandmother had been well respected. Caroline caught another glimpse of the depth of her need to reconcile the loving grandmother she thought she remembered with the years of silence she had experienced. Had her grandparents thought she wasn't good enough? That she wasn't worth bothering about? Is that why they had prayed for her but not given her a home?

CHAPTER TWO

Caroline noticed the city bus stop at the edge of the grocery store parking lot. She had located it online months ago and knew the bus taking her to the university would allow daily visits to the store on her way home from classes. Reminding herself to be careful not to buy more than she could carry, she eagerly investigated the layout of the store; and though she purchased only necessities, she was tired by the time she placed the bags on the counter at home and eased off her backpack. Her few perishables didn't seem to amount to much when deposited in the empty refrigerator, but she reminded herself that she had planned her shopping list with care and that she had done well. She was soon ready for a quick lunch in the kitchen, all the while contemplating a strategy to systematically clean cupboards while running the dishes through the dishwasher. It didn't take long to begin the process, and as soon as the dishwasher was running, she unlocked the back door and stepped into the yard. It was much too beautiful outside for her to be a dutiful housekeeper today. Besides, she was determined to be a healthy, well-rounded person.

Breathing the fresh air appreciatively, she ignored the large detached garage which she knew no longer contained her grandmother's car, and ambled around the yard. All of outdoors seemed arrayed in glorious fall colors today, bold and gold. As she progressed down the slope of the lawn and flower beds, she passed a small greenhouse with an attached garden shed. It was locked, but she remembered seeing an assortment of keys hanging on a hook in the flower room. She supposed she should call it the mudroom or the garden room or the craft room, but it would always be the flower room to her, and it would always speak of leisure and beauty, though it was not particularly attractive in itself. She would think of ways to make its appearance live up to her ideal, and to the rest of the house. As for the greenhouse, she wasn't sure she would ever make proper use of it. It seemed like an unnecessary expense right now, but someday perhaps she would learn how to make it pay for itself. She would have enjoyed a swimming pool! But realistically, she was glad that she didn't have to deal with the expense of maintaining one. It was fortunate for her that things appeared to be pretty well taken care of for the coming of winter. There was one thing she would do, someday, though. Someday, she would have the most elaborate but tasteful gazebo imaginable installed here on the edge of the woods. Someday, when she had her computer science degree, and a master's degree, and a paying job.

"Five years, tops!" she promised herself.

She mustn't lose sight of her goal or let anything hinder her. She would use that gazebo as incentive, as a very special, tangible goal. It would be the symbol of not just hanging on, but of making her contribution to the charm of the setting, building on her heritage.

Her feet automatically followed the path that wound down between raised vegetable beds carefully covered with plastic in their unplanted state. Curving into the woods, she knew the path led to a dock on the lake that she should be able to see soon. There, through the trees, she glimpsed blue water! What glorious times she would have out on the lake! The boathouse was unpretentious and, again, locked. She knew it contained only a canoe and a small rowboat. It wasn't a large lake, but was not so small either, and only half of the shore was hers. She shared the lake with the Lockwoods next door, but what an absolute treasure! It seemed to be a safe setting, stuck here between the two properties, and the Lockwoods were elderly and friendly. It was probably a good thing winter was on its way, or she would be tempted outside so often, for so long, that she wouldn't be able to keep up with her course work. She sat on the small, old-fashioned dock and let her feet dangle. They didn't quite touch the water. Should she try to get a boat in the water for the fall months? She might get it into the water, but getting it out again was another matter. Once classes began, there would be no time for boating. Besides, there would be a lot to do, just to take care of the place. She couldn't wait to get registered and begin classes at the university, but she certainly had enough to do in the meantime!

Her next challenge would be to purchase top-of-the-line computer equipment to handle all she would need in order to put herself in touch with the world academically. She had taken enough computer science courses at the junior college last year to know she wanted the ability to do some specialized, in-depth projects and was terribly afraid of how much she was going to end up spending. If only she knew enough to buy computer components and put one together herself! There was no one here she could trust to do that for her. She knew a little about hardware, but not as much as she knew about software. She couldn't afford to make mistakes, and she couldn't really afford to walk into a computer store and purchase what she knew she was going to need. And she would need it. No more hanging out in public buildings because they were more pleasant and had more resources than whatever place the courts said she should call home at the time! She was certain she would have to use the typically windowless computer labs at school for some projects, but she wanted to do as much of her work at home as possible. Home. There was that word again.

"All of this has been entrusted to me," she thought in awe.

She gazed across the lake, around the wood-trimmed shores, and up at the sky. Could she keep it, maintain it, and enjoy it but not become a slave to it? Could she make it a home?

"I refuse to let worry take the pleasure out of this," she said aloud. It would be a challenge, but worth every effort.

She strode back uphill toward the house. The acres of woods could survive on their own: that's the way it would have to be for the next few years. She would have to pay the yard crew for mowing and fertilizing the wide spreads of open lawn maybe even this fall and again throughout the next summer. It was all there in her financial plan. Emerging from the woods, she looked confidently up at the house, so solid yet so graceful. What a gift!

An undeniable curve of windows looked out toward the lake from a third floor level, tucked up under the steeply rising roofline. She had assumed there was only an unfinished attic above the second floor. This third floor area was invisible from the front of the house, but how had she missed it from the inside? The locked door in the hallway outside her grandparents' room! She had been too exhausted to worry about the key to that door last night, but remembered wondering if it led to a closet or an attic. Not an attic, a whole third floor by the look of it! She hurried up the hill and into the house. None of the keys in the flower room seemed appropriate, and besides, that wouldn't be the logical place to keep it. The study? Going through the desk drawers didn't reveal a key that looked large enough. She ran up the stairs and tried one anyway, but it didn't fit.

In her grandparents' room, she stood hesitantly surveying the plush details. Then, she opened the nearest top bedside drawer and, there, staring her in the face, was an envelope with her name on it. Unless it was addressed to some other person named Caroline, her grandmother had written to her. Excitedly, she tore it open. There was no letter, only a key inside.

It was *the* key! It fit and turned smoothly. She opened the door wide and climbed the carpeted steps. At the top was one large room, deeply carpeted, with lofted ceiling. It was a spacious area filled with light. The windows opened the room to a sweeping view of woods, lake, and sky. It was wonderful!

She stood for a long time in front of the framed high school graduation pictures of her mother and Uncle Brad, a picture of her grandfather, and one of herself as a very young child with her mother. She could hardly take her eyes from her mother's face to investigate the rest of the room. Through her tears, she finally turned to see reclining armchairs, comfortable loveseats, reading lights, display cases and bookshelves, and a beautifully carved antique walnut desk facing the view. Whereas the study downstairs was masculine and had no doubt been her grandfather's, this had obviously been her grandmother's retreat. The colors of the breakfast room were reflected here but with more intensity. Right then and there, Caroline knew that this was where she wanted to be at the close of every day for the rest of her life as the light of the setting sun mixed sky and room into one. She promised herself that it would be so, whenever it was within her power. Had her grandmother felt as strongly about this room? Had she left it specifically to Caroline because it was so special to her? Caroline was filled with gratitude and the budding knowledge of something else: in spite of all she had experienced to the contrary, she was beginning to believe her grandmother had loved her.

ও।ে

She found herself sitting, hungry eyes eating up detail after detail of the magnificent view, then more reflectively turning her gaze back to the room around her. If she were going to keep her promise to herself, she had only a few hours to accomplish as much as possible before her date with the setting sun. It was worth a try!

Back downstairs, she managed to get a professional looking notice off to the estate lawyers. They had always treated her with respect and had walked her step by step through each process, but closure felt good.

Too bad her grandparents hadn't updated their technology. Even ill old Mr. Axel had used a better computer than her grandfather's. She had taken over all of the financial records for Mr. Axel as his illness progressed. His wife had sold everything in the garage sale before she went to live with her sister, but Mr. Axel's outdated computer hadn't been close enough to what she knew she would need, even at garage sale prices. After she registered at the university tomorrow, maybe she'd have time to stop in a computer store somewhere along the way and begin to comparison shop. She had only two weeks to get organized and might need to order online to get the best possible prices. Should she put her tech center in her grandfather's study or in her grandmother's third story retreat? She wanted a study center with a lot more power than the laptop she had been using for the last year. She had a pretty good idea of what was available online, and tomorrow she would begin to find out what was available locally.

Maybe this was a good time to explore the basement. Down the stairs she flew, plans and thoughts racing through her mind as she inspected the new work that had been accomplished to update the heating and cooling. It certainly looked comprehensive. She was confident that the thermostats upstairs and the new furnaces downstairs would do their jobs. With the fall chill in the air, she hoped she could wait until next summer to try out the air conditioning.

The days might still be warm, but she would probably be in classes until late afternoon with the heavy schedule she anticipated. If a warm spell came, the basement was certainly pleasant enough and cool enough to get her through the few weeks until the weather really changed.

Her grandmother's laundry room had everything one could desire, and though she wished it had better lighting, she would think of an easy fix for that. An adjoining sewing room looked like another interesting afternoon of exploration. Stacks of fabric as well as drawers stuffed with trim, thread, buttons, and well-organized sewing supplies filled the room. Her grandmother's files of outdated patterns would probably not be of help to her, but the sewing machine, serger, and quilting machines caused her to exclaim with joy. She had thought the portable she'd purchased from Mrs. Axel would be of such great help, but here was an abundance she could hardly have imagined!

A large recreation room, bathroom, bedroom, and several storage areas completed the basement. Everything seemed to be in good shape and her grandmother must have been an impeccable housekeeper, but the construction dust from the work that had been done made Caroline glad she had decided to go ahead with the cleaning crew. The realtors would have done it again before putting the house on the market anyway, she reasoned.

Fortifying herself with a protein bar she had placed in her

very own kitchen pantry, she dragged the vacuum cleaner out of a coat closet in the front hall and vacuumed the large expanse of marble tile. The floor flowed continuously under open arches into the dining room, which took considerably longer to clean what with moving chairs and things about. She couldn't begrudge the time the gorgeous Oriental rug took to vacuum, and she knew how she'd feel if a friend of her grandmother's dropped in. Besides, she was really doing it for herself. Making her surroundings pleasant always lifted her spirits, and there was no telling how long it would be before the cleaning crew could come. She had just pulled the vacuum cleaner out of sight in the upstairs hall and started down the stairs to heat her frozen dinner when the doorbell rang. The peephole revealed that it was the neighbor lady she had spoken to that morning. Caroline reluctantly opened the door as her mind dredged up the appropriate name.

"Mrs. Lockwood, how are you?"

"Oh, please call me Martha. Since your grandmother can't be here to grandmother you, I'll just have to do as a fill-in. I've brought you some chicken hot from the oven. My husband just called and he's been delayed a few minutes, so I thought I'd take a minute and bring you some supper. I made blueberry waffles this morning and I always freeze the extras. I thought you might enjoy having a few of those as well. I just keep them in the freezer and put one on a plate with syrup to heat in the microwave. They're almost as good as fresh."

"Oh, how nice!" stammered Caroline, a little taken aback. The food looked and smelled delicious. She couldn't very well refuse chicken hot from the oven. And her favorite, blueberry waffles, to add variety to her breakfast menu this week! It would help her budget as well.

"I'm sorry. Have you eaten already? Maybe you could just save the chicken for tomorrow."

"No. No, I haven't eaten. It all looks delicious. Thank you so much. It smells wonderful!" she said, accepting the offerings.

"Now, there's one other thing I've brought that you should know about," continued Martha. "For decades, we exchanged house keys with your grandparents in case of someone being locked out or in case someone needed to let in servicemen or repair people. You know, we received packages for one another, and looked after the paper and mail for each other when we went on vacation. Millie Larson and I have just kept it up for your grandmother since her passing. I mean, when the lawyers arranged for all the work to be done, we took turns coming over and supervising. To make sure things weren't damaged. Whenever we could, we recommended people from our church that we knew were trustworthy, but we still felt we should be in the house whenever someone else was here. Your grandmother had so many beautiful things. Well anyway, I would be glad to keep the key for you in case you ever needed it. Or, if you would like, you may have it back, but I wanted to make sure you knew about it."

Martha held the key out toward Caroline who knew from experience that everyone at some time or other locked herself out. She certainly wouldn't need to fear this elderly woman and her husband. Besides, there was an additional security latch she could flip on from the inside whenever she was home. She might even be away at school sometime when there was a need for someone to get into the house, and the sudden revelation that the house and all her grandmother's possessions had been guarded by two old friends filled her with gratitude.

"Oh, Mrs. Lockwood, I would be so grateful if you kept the key. No doubt sometime or other I will need to make use of it!"

"Well, I know you don't really know me. And it is hard to trust a stranger with a key to your house, but I do hope you'll allow me to indulge myself in being a surrogate grandmother. You know they say once a mother, always a mother. And it's the same with grandmothers! I'm just so happy for Emily that you've come home," Martha said giving Caroline a quick hug. "If you ever need to get into our house and we're not at home, go to the next house down the street. They have *our* key. Now that you know what yours looks like, you'll find it hanging on a hook under my kitchen sink anytime you need it."

With another quick hug, Martha turned toward home.

"You just let me know if you need anything!"

"Only a computer!" Caroline joked.

"Oh! I'll send my grandson over! He's coming to dinner Friday. He's one of those computer whizzes. I must get dinner on the table! Bye," she said, turning and hurrying away.

"Thank you!" called Caroline.

"Oh no!" she thought, leaning against the closed door. Martha had taken her joke seriously. Now there was some unknown grandson coming to pay her a call!

She took the food to the kitchen, dutifully assigned the package of waffles to the freezer, and put the plate of food on a tray. There was a whole meal and more, more food than she could possibly eat in one sitting, so she removed the large chicken breast and stowed it in the refrigerator for lunch the next day. It would make a wonderful chicken salad sandwich and there was still plenty of chicken and a baked potato on the plate for her supper. She added a simple salad and surveyed her dinner tray hungrily.

Upstairs on the third floor sitting squarely at the desk, facing west with the tray in front of her, a picture long forgotten came into her mind of her mother and grandmother's heads bowed in prayer with her. It had been before lunch on some long-forgotten day, perhaps in the sun-filled breakfast room, in the dining room, or was it here, far above the cares of the world?

"I am grateful for this food. It's more delicious and complete than I would have done for myself," she acknowledged.

As she lifted her fork, she was struck with a vivid remembrance of her words to God that very morning. Was Martha the answer to that spontaneous prayer for people to care for her? She hadn't really expected God to answer, and all in the same day. Perhaps it was coincidence, but there was a presence in the room softly convincing her otherwise. She ate in silence, wondering again about God and her grandparents and herself.

As the sun set, Caroline decided to let go of all her questions. She knew when to enjoy a good thing. After a while she moved a chair up to the windows and sat as close as she could to gain the broadest perspective on the sky. It was glorious. Surely not every sunset would be as spectacular, but this one claimed her complete attention and drenched the room with color. She was tired and she didn't have studies to attend to, so she indulged her craving for beauty, drinking in the brilliant colors that had brought her personal peace through the years in a variety of locations and circumstances. How could mere light contain the properties for such beauty? Was God responsible for the glory of the sunset? If he had made the world, then he certainly was responsible for beauty as well. She had often wondered if he orchestrated the sunsets, but then she had wondered why he hadn't done a better job of orchestrating her life. Why had she been born? True, she had always been cared for and never harmed in spite of her many and varied moves from house to house and family to family. Was that safe protection God's doing? Tonight she could almost believe it.

When the room had grown quite gloomy, she closed the drapes and turned on the lights. This was the room that would tell her about her grandmother, and she began to explore it in earnest. The cobwebs and dust were more obvious here, the room evidently being locked away when the workmen and cleaning crew had come. Should she have the cleaning crew do this room when they came? She mustn't forget to call Mrs. Larson tomorrow in the middle of registering for classes and searching out computer stores. Now she had the added necessity of setting up her computer system before Friday so she could inform Martha that her grandson's help was unnecessary. Maybe she could just arrange to be away from home on Friday evening when he came to call.

The room contained a few expensive collectibles beautifully displayed behind glass, but the only locked case seemed to be one that contained photo albums, scrapbooks, and journals. She should have begun with the desk, of course: no doubt she would find the key to the locked bookcase there. When she pulled open the top middle drawer, she found an assortment of both lovely and practical pens and pencils along with a plain white envelope with her name handwritten on it. It very nearly matched the envelope she had found in her grandmother's nightstand, and as she tore it open a key fell onto the desk. When it opened the locked cabinet she knew that this was the key to her heritage. Her grandmother had wanted her to have it!

The photo albums were the biggest attraction and time flew by while she pored over pictures of her grandparents, her mother and Uncle Brad as children, and, yes, pictures of herself as a baby and toddler with adoring mother. She had been born into a family, a family that loved her. There were pictures of herself with doting grandparents, Emily and Jack. There were a few of her handsome father, Robert Engbert, with them, but the majority seemed to be of Caroline and her very beautiful, very young mother, Candice. These were pictures she had never known existed. Much later, a glance at the clock surprised her: it was two in the morning, yet she felt she had more questions than answers. More now than ever! The journals were the real key, but she was too exhausted to even begin. They seemed to be chronologically arranged, all written in her grandmother's elegant hand, but still it seemed overwhelming. She would have to leave them for another day, and tomorrow was full of college demands outside of her control. She replaced the albums, locked the cabinet, and placed the key in the desk before descending the stairs to prepare for bed, her head full of images. Whether the images were of photos, memories, or her own imaginings she wasn't entirely sure.

ᴥ CHAPTER THREE ᴥ

As always, a sound night's sleep brought clarification to the situation as well as the inevitable cheerfulness of an active body and mind. Caroline felt as though she had been there for a week, yet in reality she had spent only one full day in her new, old home. She knew more about her family than when she'd arrived, but there was so much more she wanted to know. It was going to take some time. Since she had come home to stay, she could afford to spend today ensuring her future. She was excited to see the university and check out all of the facilities available to her as a student. She ate quickly, thinking she would forego the Bible reading for those days to come when she had more time, but was brought up short by the fear of missing something. Yesterday had been a day of revelation. Revelation from God, or merely revelations from her life circumstances? She didn't know. How could anyone know? No one had ever seen God and no one could ever prove he existed. She turned to Day One in the study guide, and then finding the book of John in her grandmother's

Bible, she began to read John 1:1.

"In the beginning was the Word, and the Word was with God, and the Word was God. He was with God in the beginning."

The discussion and questions in the devotional guide, along with the explanatory notes in the Bible, helped her to quickly determine who the Word was. It was Jesus. What did it mean that Jesus was with God in the beginning? She continued reading John chapter one.

"Through him all things were made; without him nothing was made that has been made."

The study guide asked the question, "Do I believe that Jesus is God?" but she wasn't sure what she really thought about that. She skipped over the rest of the questions and went back to reading the Bible. It said that another man named John (John the Baptist, the devotional guide explained), came to testify about Jesus. Jesus was the light. Jesus was the origin of the world. He was rejected by his own world, the world he had created! If he had created the world, she supposed Jesus really was God. She read some of the comments and questions in the study guide for Days 2 and 3, and then went back to the Bible readings. According to verse eighteen, there was only one person who had really seen and truly been with God, and it was Jesus, the one who had come to make the Father known.

Jesus had seen God! He came from God's very presence

in heaven to tell us about God the Father and was now seated at the Father's side. What did it mean that we could be born into God's family? Caroline had been rejected by her family, hadn't she? Perhaps she knew how Jesus felt, being rejected by his own world. Could she become part of God's family? Would God reject her, turn from her, and leave her in silence as her family had? Did God truly love her? Had her parents and grandparents truly loved her? The years of silence and abandonment had built an obstacle tall and wide. Her mind churning anew, she told herself she must set all of this aside for now. She dared not continue these upsetting thoughts. She had work to do.

It was still early, though she had started another load of dishes and packed a lunch for the day, and the air was brisk as she walked the six blocks to the bus stop. Thanks in part to Martha's wonderful cooking, she wouldn't need to stop at the store today.

The bus ride to the university was interesting and seemed to pass quickly as she eagerly scanned the new territory lining the streets. She noted a drycleaner, a delicious looking bakery, and several other interesting looking stores along the way. There was a computer store which she didn't particularly like the looks of, but determined to stop at on her way home.

It took some time, with standing in the inevitable lines and clearing up the inevitable questions in the registrar's office, to make sure that they would allow her to register for the classes she needed. They had received her transfer credits from high school AP courses and the credits she had taken last year while she sorted out the complexities of Mr. Axel's passing, Mrs. Axel's future, and her own out-of-the-blue inheritance. If all went according to plan, she would register as a junior next semester. Setting her sights on early graduation would condense her remaining undergraduate time to two years. Could she do it? There was one computer science course she had missed out on, so her load this fall would be extra heavy. Even with the scholarship she had been awarded that cut her tuition in half, the bill she paid for the semester's tuition seemed frightening. She reminded herself to look on it as an investment in her future. Thanks to a combination of her own academic scholarship and her grandparents' money, she was officially enrolled without going into debt!

Some courses required downloads, but several books were also required and she wanted to make sure she had everything before classes began. The bookstore was a madhouse. She eventually managed to find all of her textbooks, many of them used but still enormously expensive, and finally inched her way through the line to the cash register. She paid for her books, thanks again to her grandparents, and stepped out into the sunshine for a deep breath of fresh air. Textbooks could have waited until next week, but she didn't want to make unnecessary trips to campus. There would be bus fare to pay, too much to do at home before classes began, and the possibility of the bookstore running out of what she needed. Characteristically, she liked to get a head start on her classes, and she needed to be ready for a particularly heavy course load. Next semester she would try to purchase everything online well ahead of time. She drifted across the campus looking for a peaceful, pleasant place to eat her lunch. A stone wall, set in an expanse of lawn, was shaded from the sun's midday warmth by a maple tree and offered her just the seat she was looking for. She had wrapped her chicken salad (compliments of Martha) in a neat package of red lettuce rather than bread which, along with an apple and perusal of several of her textbooks, made for a pleasant lunch.

Consulting her campus map before hoisting her heavy pack, she started off in the direction of the computer science buildings. She had arranged to meet her advisor and ask his opinion about purchasing computer equipment that would help her meet future course requirements. Even though she had signed up for an appointment, there was another student with him when she arrived, and knowing how much time he was most likely giving to new students like herself today, she was relieved when he waved her into his office after twenty minutes. Dr. Calton seemed pleasant enough and willing to help if she needed anything. He obligingly recommending a computer store two blocks from campus in the opposite direction from her bus stop and discussed features she would need if she wanted to complete her degree while working at home as much as possible. Of course, there were labs she was welcome to use on campus, and certain projects would require use of systems beyond what she would have access to on her own. However, for what she would need, he said that both faculty and students frequented the store he had recommended, and that she should mention his name. He was sure they would give her a fair market price, but she was dismayed when he mentioned the price ranges. He also mentioned some online sites she already knew about that might have better deals. Caroline thought of her dwindling nest egg but knew she couldn't work and take extra courses at the same time. She had to succeed! If she had to get a part time job, she would talk to him about it later when the need arose.

Instead, she explained the senior project she had in mind and asked for advice on resources she would need to accomplish what she wanted.

"Fascinating!" Dr. Calton exclaimed, quirking an eyebrow at her. "It's an ambitious project, but if you get started now, it would be possible."

"Can you get me access?"

"I think so. Check with me after class the first week."

"Great! Thanks!"

Caroline had gotten up to leave when she noticed a

calendar on the wall, this month's picture displaying the glory of the stars of the Milky Way. At the bottom of the picture she recognized with a jolt the words she had read that very morning in John. "Through him all things were made," declared the caption, and, somehow, it settled one question then and there. Yes, God, creator of such a vast display of starry beauty was believably responsible for the light and color display of the sunset. Her advisor couldn't help but notice that the calendar had caught her attention.

"Do you recognize the words?" Dr. Calton asked.

"Yes. I mean, I read them this morning I think."

"Is it your habit to read the Bible? Are you a Christian?" he asked with interest.

"Yes. No. I mean, I only just started reading John."

"So, are you a Christian or are you searching for something? For God?"

"I… I thought everyone was a Christian. I mean, you are aren't you?" Caroline asked in confusion.

"Yes, I am, but only because I've been born into God's family. If you keep reading John you're sure to find out what it really means to become a Christian."

"Uh… well thanks. I guess I'd better head over to that computer store."

"Come and see me again anytime. I'd like to hear about your progress in John."

"Thanks! See you in class."

She had plenty to think about for two blocks, the weight of her backpack forgotten. She'd always thought this God thing was a private thing. Dr. Calton didn't treat it that way. How strange to see those words on that calendar and to hear Dr. Calton talk about being born into God's family. Wasn't she a Christian after all? She'd always tried to do the right thing. Was there something else she had to do? She hadn't chosen her family. Did she have to choose God's family? How?

She browsed her way around the computer store, mentioned that she was a student of Dr. Calton's, and soon had a firm quote on what she needed. Unfortunately, it was in the price range she had expected. Thanking the employee, she left the store, making her way back toward campus and her bus stop. She walked through several buildings on the way just to become more familiar with the campus, and took a detour to include a couple of the computer labs and the library. Normally she would have checked out a good prospect or two for bedtime reading from the fiction section in spite of the weight of her pack, but those journals of her grandmother's would absorb her reading time, and the house was literally filled with literature of exceptional quality. She had noticed titles and authors that she had read and many she hadn't, all in handsome editions, enough to fulfill any urge to read that she could possibly experience in the coming months. Actually, it was a good thing she wouldn't be adding to the weight of her backpack with the inevitable recreational reading. No matter how busy she was, she almost always found time for reading, and she looked forward to becoming well acquainted with her grandparents' bookshelves. This semester, however, she suspected her reading would be limited to required course content.

She sank into her bus seat with relief and eased off her pack. All too soon, the stop approached for the computer store she had noticed on the way to the university that morning.

"No stone unturned," she thought as she swung her pack on again and hopped off the bus. The store was dark and dirty, and she didn't like the way the clerk looked her over. She quickly stated her business and could tell the clerk was weighing how much he could charge her. He wanted her to think she was getting a good price because he liked her, but his greed was a definite factor. He talked as though he were the owner. The price he finally disclosed when she pressed for a direct answer was considerably more than the other store's quote. She left the store as soon as possible, feeling very uncomfortable. Wanting to put as much distance between herself and the man in the store, she walked briskly along the bus route to the next stop. She would never get off at that stop again if she had any choice in the matter.

When the bus deposited her at her own stop, she was reminded of the need to call Mrs. Larson.

"Hi, Caroline! Please call me Millie. Your grandmother was such a dear friend. Martha and I are so pleased that you're living in your grandparents' home. We'll just have to be surrogate grandparents too. Two sets for the price of one!"

"That's very kind of you, Mrs. Larson. Millie. I guess I need to thank you for taking care of the house. Martha told me you sometimes came over to keep an eye on things."

"Oh, yes. But you know I did it for Emily, and I didn't know *you* then, but I'm happy I did it for you too."

"Thank you. I really appreciate coming and finding everything in such good shape. Were you able to arrange for a cleaning crew? I shouldn't have asked you to do it. I'm sorry to take up your time."

"Nonsense, My Dear! They're coming Tuesday at nine, a crew of four, so we can put two to work upstairs and two in the basement or downstairs."

"Oh, thanks so much. That will be wonderful."

"Of course you'll have to pay them, but I also have a crew of four or five ladies from church and we'd like to come and clean your kitchen for you, just for the fun of it. We'd so love to have a chance to meet you. I'm sure it must seem overwhelming! Emily had such a wonderful kitchen, but I'm sure everything must need cleaning."

"Oh, oh no! You don't have to do that!"

"Nonsense. We'd love to do it! I can't wait to meet you. My doorbell's ringing, so I'll say goodbye. We'll be there bright and early, before the cleaning crew. See you Tuesday!"

Caroline drew in a sharp breath to reply, but Millie was gone and there was no one to hear Caroline's frustrated groan. So much for her plan to live quietly and anonymously. She was going to be invaded on Tuesday! If there was one thing she did not want, it was a bunch of strangers, women, from a church, in her kitchen! A cleaning crew was impersonal and professional: they came in, did their job, and left. Caroline had never felt she had much in common with housewives or groups of gabby women. She had always pretty much been a loner.

"And that's how I like it," she thought to herself, pushing aside the memory of yesterday's lonely cry for people to care for her. It wasn't fair! She wanted to choose the people and the times she would allow them into her life, and this was not what she'd had in mind.

Depositing her heavy backpack in the family room, she realized this was where she would need to do her studying. Her computer center would have to go here in the easily-accessible main floor study. She would save the third floor for dreaming. She walked into her grandfather's study to decide where and how to set up a whole new system in an old-fashioned room that had never been intended for technology. The dark wood paneling and heavy furniture were rich and masculine in appearance. She didn't want to change the mood of the room. She loved the strong, deep colors, and she certainly didn't want to ruin the view from the desk, a classic sweep of stone patio and sloping lawn through French doors, a smaller version of the view from the adjacent family room.

The desk was large. She just might be able to stow all of the necessary network components on top, underneath, in, and around the desk. It was easy to follow the electrical cords to the outlet which was located inobtrusively in the floor beside the desk. Could she hide the outlet under the desk and add a power strip to plug everything into? She tried lifting the end of the desk and couldn't budge it, so found herself hoping there would be some men in that cleaning crew on Tuesday.

Since tomorrow was Friday, she would check a few more computer stores, making sure that she wasn't home around dinnertime when Martha's grandson might show up. Or maybe she should ask him to help her move the desk. No. She didn't really want Martha's grandson feeling at home in her house. For all she knew, he might well be more acquainted with it than she was!

She spent some time cleaning out the desk and emptying areas she might need. It would take hours to shred the papers and cumbersome ledgers that reflected various accounts. She had the current information she needed about her various assets on her laptop, and she hoped to soon be tracking all of her financial transactions on her new computer, with a separate backup hard drive as well. Mr. Axel's assets had not been as great as hers now were, but it had been good practice to manage his, and she was confident that she knew what she was doing. The number of drawers, cabinets, and shelves that she had not even investigated were a source of frustration. Thankfully, the study and family room had been closed up and were easily made presentable with a surface dusting. She wanted so badly to go upstairs and begin reading journals! That reminded her of another question she'd been avoiding. Did she want the third floor cleaned on Tuesday, or should she do it herself? Had her grandmother ever allowed people in her retreat, or had she taken care of it personally? Why not just lock the door and keep it private? But then she'd have to clean it all herself.

She was feeling a bit overwhelmed again with all that she was attempting to do when the doorbell rang. A quick glance revealed that the last of her belongings had been delivered, and she suddenly found herself with three large boxes to unpack and put away somewhere. She couldn't start the school year feeling like she was camping out in someone else's room. Her room would have to take priority, other than getting the computer network up and running.

So Caroline deposited Mrs. Axel's portable sewing machine in the basement sewing room and spent the remainder of the evening moving odds and ends out of her room into other bedroom closets and dressers, finding and setting aside a few of her mother's personal belongings in the process. She took the time only to warm a frozen dinner and catch the sunset, which was not as spectacular as the previous night. Cleaning her room as she went along, by bedtime she was happy with the results. The room was arranged in a way that suited her, she liked the furnishings, and she had arranged her clothes conveniently for easy use. It was a wonderful feeling. Grimy and weary, she thoroughly enjoyed her second shower of the day before retrieving the oldest journal she could find and climbing into bed. Tomorrow she would have to do some laundry, but now that she had a place to put it away, she could put all else from her mind and focus on her family, her own past!

Grandmother Emily's journal entries began with the birth of her son. Brad's coming was such a miracle from God that she was moved to begin recording her feelings and experiences. Some entries were long, many were short, and there were gaps of days, weeks, even months, but Caroline read with pleasure all the joys of her grandparents' new family. Caroline's own mother, Candice, soon joined them, and many special occasions, holidays, and family trips described happy times after her birth. There were undercurrents though, times when Grandmother Emily poured out her heart, revealing that she had married Jack against her parents' wishes, and even against God's wishes. Jack was not a "believer," and grew increasingly opposed to Emily's church attendance, friendships, and connections. He resented being left alone on Sunday mornings and refused to accompany Emily and the children to church, making it more and more unpleasant for Emily. As the children grew, Jack's desire for little Brad to "be a man" constituted emotional abuse at times, confusing and hurting Uncle Brad's spirit. To Brad, Jack sometimes held up religion as something for the weak and abnormal. How Emily hurt for her young son and the hardness, the unkindness, that she saw growing within him! And yet she held their little family together, forgiving Jack, praying for him, and asking God to forgive him and save him.

God, please have mercy on Jack. He doesn't know what he's doing to his children. Please bring Jack into your family, your kingdom. Please bring Brad to the point that he can accept you, Jesus, and what you've done for him. Please let Candice's heart soften to the Gospel while she is young. Let them each learn that you love them so much you gave your life so they can live.

Caroline fell asleep with her grandmother's prayers running through her thoughts. Did God really answer prayer?

❧ CHAPTER FOUR ❧

Friday morning was the opportune time to start a load of laundry and do some ironing before her stomach demanded breakfast. It didn't take long for both a good start on her wardrobe and for her healthy appetite to kick in. She would save Martha's waffles to thoroughly enjoy when she had more time, but no more instant oatmeal! She had purchased the real thing at the natural grocer's. Her hands caressed the smooth surface of Grandmother's blue and white Spode dishes. She couldn't help but appreciate the fineness of the informal Geranium pattern. Placing a few frozen blueberries in the bottom of her bowl and filling it with hot oatmeal, she took it to the breakfast room with a cup of tea. How different this was from her previous experiences with breakfast! As the blueberries warmed and the oatmeal cooled and approached eating temperature, she picked up her grandmother's Bible. The next verses in the book of John spoke of Jesus being baptized in water, but also of John saying that Jesus would baptize with God's spirit. John called

Jesus the Lamb of God, the Son of God, and Andrew called him the Messiah, the Christ. Caroline learned from the study guide that Jesus was called the Lamb of God because, just like the innocent lambs which were sacrificed to cover sin in Old Testament times, so Jesus was sacrificed on the cross to cover our sins. Sins!

"I'm not so bad," she thought.

Her sins didn't amount to much, did they, especially since she had managed to grow up on her own and turn into a responsible, functioning adult? Avoiding the pitfalls other teens seemed so easily to fall into had been a lonely path, but she intended to make something of her life! She still felt uneasy about this whole sin thing. Brushing her feelings aside, she realized this explained why there were cute little lamb drawings associated with Easter: it was not because of spring but because Jesus was the Lamb, the sacrifice or offering provided by God for everyone! She'd heard of Peter, of course, so it was interesting to read about Jesus renaming him Peter, meaning "rock." The study guide said it was based on what he would later become in the church. So Jesus had known all about Peter, and as she read to the end of the first chapter it seemed Jesus had known all about Nathanael being a good person. Then Jesus must know that *she* was a good person.

Why did Jesus call himself the "Son of Man?" It evidently referred back to someone named Daniel (of Daniel in the lion's den fame!) who had prophesied 500 years earlier that someone who looked like a son of man (human) was going to be given all power by God so that people would worship this son of man and he would have a kingdom that would last forever. She didn't really understand, but as she went back to reread John chapter one and to read more of the study guide, she learned that Jesus was God, but born as a man, like all of us and yet sinless, the only one of us ever to be sinless. The guide referred her to Romans 3:23 which said, "for all have sinned and fall short of the glory of God." She went thoughtfully about her work that morning, wondering if perhaps her sin did count in God's eyes. It wasn't a pleasant feeling, and she kept remembering times when she hadn't done the right thing, times when people had been hurt and offended by her stubborn independence. Her words and actions seemed harsh now, as they came to mind.

Tired of being indoors, she collected all the keys she could find in the flower room and set out to explore the greenhouse with its shed and the boathouse, which added up to all of her outdoor holdings other than the garage. The storage shed was filled with old yard and garden tools, mostly still in good shape, and an old lawn mower that looked small and light. She supposed there might be times when she would want to clean up an area of the yard. There was no way she could mow the entire yard with it. It would take all day. She reluctantly surrendered any thoughts of saving money on the yard crew. She would concentrate on growing as much of her food as she could next summer. That would be a big enough job. And fun!

The greenhouse was a gem. It looked as though it hadn't been used in some time, but everything was neat and ready to go, even in the attached potting shed. There was obviously running water: hoses snaked through the greenhouse and a deep, rustic sink had a place inside the potting area. The water must come from the well on the property, she realized, spotting a switch labeled "pump." She turned on a faucet but got no response. The electricity was on, but she wasn't about to mess up a whole pumping system because she didn't know what she was doing, so she decided not to try the pump. Perhaps Martha or her husband would know something about it. As she turned to go, Caroline noticed with dismay that there appeared to be heating ducts running from a gas heater in the shed out to the greenhouse. Would she have to heat the greenhouse? Surely it had been closed up and made secure before last winter, but did she need to keep water pipes from freezing this winter? Was there a separate heating system out here that had remained distinct from the new furnace system? She didn't remember any conversations with the lawyers about the greenhouse. Maybe Martha Lockwood could tell her what needed to be done.

She sprinted down the path to the lake. It was wonderful to be out of doors, and it felt so good to run! The sight of serene lake water framed by the sunny picturesque setting spoke to something within her. It seemed quiet and peaceful, but as she sat observing, she realized there was a considerable amount of movement and activity going on. Birds called and dipped above the lake. The water lapped gently, interrupted here and there with spreading circles. Insects or fish? She could see raccoon tracks in the sand at the edge of the lake. She wondered if there were deer. She was glad it wasn't human activity: the Lockwood's house and boathouse were out of sight, blocked by the woods. Sometime, she promised herself, she would spend a sunset here at the lake, quietly watching to see if any wildlife showed itself. Not tonight. Tonight she would stay away in order to avoid Martha's grandson.

She stood to examine the boathouse. It really would need painting next summer. The lights responded as she flipped the big switch by the door, turning the dark cave into an enticing adventure. Both boats were high and dry and would have to stay that way until next spring. Once spring arrived for certain, she knew she would use them through the summer and figure out how to stow them in the fall when the time came. But for now, she repeated to herself that she was about to have too much studying to do.

There was a lovely old weeping willow beside the boathouse and she lingered, identifying as many trees and plants as she could along the pleasant walk back to the house.

In the distance on both sides of the path, she could see blue and green spruce mixed with long and short needled pines, an evergreen ruffle extending just above the deciduous trees. Like those protecting trees, encircling the property, she was here to stay and protect her inheritance. As she meandered back up the path, she could roughly distinguish the maples, elms, and ashes that filled the woods, each a different color and shape from the other. Back at the house, she wiped out the big desk in her grandfather's study and polished it until it shone. Hopefully within the next few days she'd be bringing home the computer network that would transform it into the center of her academic existence and the basis for her future career. She could always carry a laptop upstairs to watch the sunset, but she needed a reliable desktop, backup system, server, scanner, and the ability to print. She would have to wait and see how many other bells and whistles she could afford. There would always be new software and hardware coming out later, and she would always need updates, but she meant to start out with the best she could afford without being extravagant. After all, she didn't want a job: she wanted to pour herself into her classes.

She had been able to locate a few computer stores in the area, but getting a quote over the phone proved to be problematic. Those who seemed to be giving her a price based on reality took an eternity to do so, but she finally had two fairly comprehensive quotes that underbid the store recommended by Dr. Calton. She would have to go see if they really had what they claimed they had.

Long bus rides involving transfers helped her get to know the city, but ate up the afternoon. It was nearly suppertime before she confirmed that the second quote was a true quote, as opposed to the first one she had checked out, and that it did indeed include most of what she needed. She wished she could carry it all home on the spot, which was impossible. She'd have to pay a delivery fee, which she regretted but could see no way around. They were out of the particular printer she wanted but they expected to get more at the beginning of the week, so she would have to call next week to see if it had come in. And, some of the components would have to be transferred from other stores. It would take a few days. Frustrated, she left the store without completing the transaction and walked down the street to a nearby shopping mall where she picked up a few things she needed and found an irresistibly inexpensive fall sweater that fit her perfectly. She could definitely use it, and her thoughts were happy as she ate the cheapest items on the menu at the fast food restaurant. Water was free, including refills, she reflected philosophically.

She regretted missing the sunset, took a wrong bus, and was cold, tired, and hungry again by the time she let herself in the front door. She didn't like taking buses after dark. As a rule, she tried to do all of her business within commuter hours when the streets were well populated. Not being out alone late at night was one reason she hoped to do as much of her work as possible at home rather than in the school library and computer labs. She had just hung up her coat and brushed her hair when the doorbell rang.

She couldn't pretend she wasn't home, having just turned on the lights. A glance through the peephole showed half a pie in the hands of a masculine stranger. Martha's grandson. She supposed he was safe. The light of the open door fell on one of the handsomest young men she had ever seen. He was tall, but not too tall, trim with broad shoulders and an athletic build to match hers. Brown hair and hazel eyes complimented a ruggedly-handsome, clean-shaven face. A few years older than herself, he was, no doubt, accustomed to young women falling at his feet. Well, she would not be one of them.

"Hello," he said almost apologetically. "I'm Peter Berkhardt. John and Martha Lockwood's grandson from next door. Grandmother thought you could use the pie?"

The question mark in his voice begged her to understand. He had refused this job several times during the course of the evening, but his grandmother had insisted and one did not refuse a well-intentioned grandmother even if one smelled a well-intentioned set up. Friends and family frequently introduced him to girls, when they could arrange to do so, but he had been surprised at his grandmother's insistence.

She didn't usually participate in efforts to match Peter up with a "nice" girl. Why this one? He had childhood memories of being slightly terrified of this girl's grandfather. He had certainly been an old curmudgeon, but Peter's grandparents had said something tonight about the grandfather coming to the Lord late in his life and going through a dramatic change. They didn't seem to know if the granddaughter, Caroline, knew the Lord or not. Well, it wasn't his concern. Better to leave that to his grandparents. It was a good thing his doctoral program was engrossing and kept him miles away, allowing for only occasional visits. He had finally set out with the pie tonight intending to have as little as possible to do with his grandparents' new next-door neighbor.

His plan to leave the pie and beat a quick retreat evaporated when the door opened and he found himself looking into brown eyes unlike any he had seen before, or at least remembered seeing before. The strength and independence of spirit he read there belied her petite, almost frail beauty. Suddenly he wanted to shelter this girl from anyone or anything that would harm her. He had never before wanted so badly to care for and protect another person. What had he gotten himself into? She was pretty, too pretty. She didn't need anyone to take care of her, her eyes said, least of all him. So, with a knee-jerk prayer toward heaven for deliverance from a feeling like he had been slugged in the stomach, he introduced himself.

"Grandmother thought you were looking for a computer?" he continued.

"Oh, you don't need to worry about it. I found everything I was looking for at a good price."

"What were you looking for?"

It was easy to talk to him about her days of comparison shopping because she could tell by his questions that he knew a whole lot more about it than she did. Still, she was glad that she could say she did not require his assistance.

"I think I can get you the same set-up for about two thirds the cost. Maybe less. I have a friend who owns a computer store and he owes me a favor," Peter explained.

It was hard to refuse saving that much money.

"Oh, really?" she replied, unsure.

"I'm staying with my parents, here in town, this weekend. I could pick you up in the morning and drive you out there just to see what we could come up with."

"Uh…"

"Nine o'clock okay?" he asked.

"Sure. Thanks," she replied.

"See you at nine. Enjoy the pie," he said gesturing toward the plate in her hands. "It's blackberry. My favorite. Nobody makes it like Grandma Lockwood!"

"Thanks!"

She found herself smiling as she closed the door, then

found herself wondering why she had agreed to go with him in the morning. She never went out with strangers, especially handsome ones. What had she been thinking? Was he as trustworthy as he seemed? She would find out tomorrow. Perhaps his friend couldn't really provide such an unreasonably good deal, but it was worth checking out. She took the pie to the kitchen, made a cup of tea, and took a tray up to her room where she read journal entries until her eyes just wouldn't stay open any longer. A good night's sleep was in order to be able to think clearly about such a major purchase tomorrow. One thing was certain, Peter was right about his grandmother's blackberry pie!

❦

Climbing into Peter's car the next morning seemed awkward at first, but they found plenty to talk about and Peter took a few short detours to show her interesting local sights along the way. The computer store was busy and informally chaotic, but Peter's friend knew his stuff and soon the car was full of everything she had worked so hard to track down over the last few days. She had saved hundreds of dollars. He had even promised to keep his eyes open for bargains on things she didn't consider to be necessities. Caroline was excited and happy as they started home, then suddenly embarrassed.

"I hope I didn't use up all of his indebtedness to you. I really appreciate it."

"Not to worry."

"But maybe you could have used some discounts yourself, and I've used up all your bargaining chips."

"No, really. Don't worry. I'm all set up. He'll fix me up if I ever do need anything. Now we'd better get this home and up and running so you're ready for classes, right?"

"Yes, but you shouldn't have offered to save me so much money doing all the set up and installations yourself."

"Well, if all goes well, it shouldn't take too long to put it together. You realize, of course, my fingers are crossed behind my back so that I'm not guilty of lying. You never know how long it will really take, but I'm fairly certain it will be pretty straightforward."

They discussed software, computers, schools, and degrees all the way home, perhaps because neither one wished to get into uncomfortably personal topics of conversation. By the time they were unloading computer components and carrying them into the study, both had a healthy respect for the other. Caroline didn't once question his presence and advice, and Peter never once revealed how deep his desire was to protect Caroline like he would one of his grandmother's delicate crystal treasures. In fact, he refused to reflect on it until later, managing to keep the atmosphere friendly and relaxed with a sense of fun and good humor throughout the process of installing cards, memory, and software. They stopped only to order pizza for a late lunch, and worked well as a team, enjoying each other's company so much that they both secretly regretted that it all went together so smoothly. By dinnertime everything was working without a hitch, largely due to Peter's muscle, skill, and technical knowledge.

"How can I ever thank you?" she asked, not expecting an answer.

"Come to church and Sunday dinner with us tomorrow," he answered impulsively. "Grandmother especially wanted me to invite you."

"I… I couldn't. I have so much to do!"

"One rests on Sunday, you know. Besides, Grandmother thought you might want to see the church your grandparents went to."

"Oh. Well, maybe. I… I don't know much about church." He might as well know the worst about her.

"That's okay. I'll pick you up at eight-thirty in the morning. And if I know Grandma, she's got a roast in the refrigerator that'll be a work of art by the time church is out."

So Caroline found herself carefully, even nervously, dressing on an early Sunday morning to go to church with Peter. He explained that his parents attended a different church that was closer to their home across town, but she was introduced to Peter's grandfather, as well as the Larsons. The whole of the college group received her warmly, though at her coming many young ladies regretfully wrote off any hope of a future with the attractive, intelligent, fun, and very promising Peter Berkhardt. Of course Caroline remained blissfully ignorant of that fact, determined as she was to expect only cool, professional friendship from Peter. She met other university students who invited her to group outings planned for that month, sat through Sunday school and church where she spotted her advisor, Dr. C, as Dr. Calton was familiarly known, and heard the gospel clearly presented for the first time in her life.

"The word 'gospel' means 'good news.' The bad news is that none of us can do enough good things to be acceptable to God. But the good news of the gospel is that God himself made a way for us to be acceptable to him. God sent his only Son, Jesus, to die in our place. Jesus' perfect goodness and obedience to God's will was demonstrated by the fact that he gave his life up for us. This perfect, ultimate sacrifice for sin made a way for God to set aside our sin so that we can be restored to him," explained the preacher. "We can have access to God and his love anytime, anywhere, for all eternity, just by believing this good news, by believing God."

Before Caroline had time to digest the events of the morning, they were back at Peter's grandparents' home, praying over and then partaking of a most delicious meal that lived up to every boast of Peter on his grandmother's behalf.

Caroline and Peter helped in the kitchen with the cleaning up after the meal. Then Peter, needing to stop at his parents' before making the long drive back to his apartment and studies in another city, walked her home, saying goodbye briefly and awkwardly with her thanks ringing in his ears and her face etched in his mind where it refused to fade.

As for Caroline, it was more than she could process. She retired to her room for a nap rather than analyze any of her feelings about the totally unexpected weekend she had just experienced. She wanted to avoid thinking about any of it, from the perfect computer setup she had not thought she could afford, the genteel functionality of her study, and a morning at church she would normally never have experienced, to the large number of people that somehow now seemed part of her life, not the least of which was Peter Berkhardt.

✥ CHAPTER FIVE ✥

Caroline spent happy hours the next day at her very own computer network trying out new software and working out the bugs. Reading her grandmother's journals took up the remainder of her waking hours.

Brad agreed to go to church camp this week. Please, God, help him to find you this week, before his teen years lead him away from you!

Brad seems so different. He seems so happy!

But Grandmother had watched the joy in his eyes fade as his father's ridicule and scorn continued day after day. How her grandmother had cried out to God on her son's behalf, seemingly without effect! Brad grew tougher and more cynical, and withdrew from his mother in order to live up to his father's expectations. Caroline's heart hurt, along with her grandmother's, for this Uncle Brad she had never known and for this grandmother who loved her children and poured out her heart to God in her journal writings. Why hadn't God answered those prayers? Perhaps he had. She would keep reading.

She wasn't sure what to expect when the doorbell rang on Tuesday morning. Her two surrogate grandmothers breezed in with generous pans of lasagna to bake for everyone's lunch. They proceeded to set the cleaning crew to work after consulting with Caroline. The four ladies from their church brought additional food to complete the lunch and were soon busy in the kitchen doing what would have taken Caroline weeks to do. It wasn't until everyone was busy with assigned tasks that Millie and Martha drew Caroline aside and explained that they had often visited her grandmother in her private third story retreat and would love to help her put it in order.

"Such a lovely room with such wonderful collections from around the world," mused Millie. "Your grandfather only brought her the best, of course. But then she decided to sell several pieces at the end, when she became ill."

"Yes, God did provide for her needs even after Jack died," Martha said.

"We brought vacuums and dust cloths and paper towels and glass cleaner," recited Millie, trying to lift the mood. "Emily would want you to enjoy that room. It was very special to her."

"I already love it," Caroline replied with a smile. "It's very special to me too."

"Your grandmother didn't normally bring other people onto the third floor. She really did keep it as a private retreat. Your grandfather had it built for her when it was only the two of them left, you know."

Caroline didn't know, but she let it pass and accompanied them upstairs where she entered into the rebirth of her grandmother's retreat with a deep appreciation for these two women who, like elderly guardian angels, seemed to genuinely care about her well-being and happiness. She wondered that she didn't resent their presence.

The three of them worked hard with encouraging results, again accomplishing in one morning what would have taken her weeks to do by herself. Caroline did all of the climbing and high cleaning, and everything that required strength, but Martha and Millie contributed more than their share, despite their age. They seemed to have no interest in the cabinet full of journals, respecting her grandmother's privacy, but they recalled gently and joyfully the many times they had prayed with her grandmother and of the Lord's blessings when her grandfather had finally become a new creature in Christ. How it had changed him and how different he had been! Caroline listened with all her heart in her ears. God had answered her grandmother's prayers after all!

"Remember when Jack brought the masks from Venice,

Millie?" asked Martha as she dusted one of a pair of elaborate masks, one for a woman, one for a man.

"Oh, yes!" she laughed.

"They were very expensive, gold leaf, but I think your grandmother never really liked them," Martha confided to Caroline.

"They were quite the rage in Venice, evidently," explained Millie, "so they made the perfect souvenir. Remember how hard it was for Emily to find a way to display them?"

"Yes," laughed Martha. "She tried hanging them on the wall but they seemed to follow her around the room."

"I'm not terribly fond of them myself," admitted Caroline. "I'm glad Grandmother found a way to arrange them in the display case. I had no idea they were covered in gold leaf!"

"The gems are real, too, Caroline. I suppose you could sell the masks if you don't care for them. Emily wouldn't mind!" said Martha.

"I'm sure Jack would not object now either!" laughed Millie.

Caroline looked sober, wondering if her grandparents knew and approved of her presence in the house.

"Do you think they know I'm here?" she asked.

"No one really knows how much God reveals of our life to those who've gone to heaven. Perhaps nothing, but perhaps because they prayed for it for so many years, God would let them know he answered their prayers and brought you here. I'd like to think so," mused Martha.

Caroline steered the conversation in another direction, uncomfortable with how close they were coming to her own history. How much did Martha and Millie know about her mother and father and her own childhood? She wasn't ready to ask them that question. She'd rather know more about it herself first.

"Jack brought her so many wonderful gifts. She really did enjoy many of these beautiful pieces," Millie reflected as she dusted. "But the best gift he gave her was when he gave his life to Jesus and accepted God's gift of salvation."

"It really changed Jack," agreed Martha. "They were such a cute couple after that. So… contented. Jack had retired and they went everywhere together for the time he had left. It made Emily very happy."

"Oh, look, Martha!" exclaimed Millie. "Remember this?"

As her grandmother's two friends reminisced, Caroline learned more about her family than she would have had she asked. Her helpers seemed to know the origin of many of the objects in the room, as well as the rest of the house, and Caroline absorbed the history of each piece with interest, along with anecdotes of her family she could not have discovered in any other way. She found herself wanting Millie and Martha to come back again, to be part of her life. They were a link to her family and her heritage.

Lunch was fun, Caroline decided, surprising herself by enjoying a kitchen table crowded with these people who were mostly strangers to her. They joked and laughed as though they enjoyed giving their time, some for pay and some not, just for the joy of being together and cleaning her house. A couple more hours of work would have to do it. Many of them had other obligations for the day, so a battle plan was laid out and the work divided. At the end of the day they filed out of the door with vacuum cleaners and cleaning supplies, leaving behind visible evidence of their well wishes. Caroline closed the door and leaned against it. She was exhausted but happy. Never would she have chosen to let these people into her life, but she couldn't argue with the results, and she had genuinely enjoyed having them in her home. She had thanked them each, making sure they knew she deeply appreciated what they had done.

The entry hall now shone and sparkled, as did the rest of the house visible from where she stood by the front door. She could never repay all of them, but she could have Millie and Martha and their husbands over for dinner before school began. What fun to entertain in her own home! It was the least she could do, as long as she made it clear she could not keep up this pace of socializing once she became a full-time student. She wandered through the house, taking pleasure in each room. One of the girls in the cleaning crew had agreed to come for a reasonable rate if Caroline ever needed someone for an hour or two to help. It seemed too good to be true that she could expect to live in such elegant cleanliness and order!

In the library, she sat at the beautiful grand piano and played out of joy rather than need. How often the piano had been her solace. Not tonight. Tonight was for rejoicing.

❧❧

The remainder of the week was filled with reading the Gospel of John from her grandmother's Bible in the mornings and long, busy days ending with late-night journal reading. She had issued her invitation to the Larsons and the Lockwoods for the following week, setting herself on a course of meal planning along with table and flower arranging which she thoroughly enjoyed. She had never known how much fun it could be to arrange a dinner for people she wanted to thank. The butler's pantry became a rewarding source of delicate, tasteful china and glassware, all of which she handled carefully and appreciatively as she decided which pieces to use for her dinner party.

She jogged through the neighborhood, meeting a few other neighbors and learning her way around, and made a trip to the store Thursday for her menu items. She spent quiet daylight and dusk moments at the lake and in Grandmother's retreat. She wondered about God and his kindness toward her and the puzzle that was her life; and, despite her best efforts, more than once she wondered if she would ever hear from Peter Berkhardt. He was busy, of course. His classes had already begun. He had never said she would hear from him. She did not have his address or phone number, and he would have no reason to contact her. They had merely spent a day together assembling her tech needs and he had taken her to church at his grandparents' request. Perhaps he had a girlfriend, or at least many friends who were girls. Were they in a social set to which she didn't belong? She felt comfortable with the group at church, but somehow she had gotten the impression that his parents were very wealthy. Perhaps, in spite of her grandparents' house, she didn't seem to belong to this gracious class of people. Or was it that she wasn't what they would call a real Christian?

As for Peter, he returned to school thankful that his remaining year of doctoral work would be demanding, rigorous, and all consuming. It was not easy to put Caroline Engbert out of his mind. He had a deep desire for her to come to know the Lord Jesus Christ as her Savior, a desire he did not trust himself to pursue. He knew that it needed to happen independently of his influence and he knew that he needed to stay away from Caroline until she had made that decision and become a child of God. If he spent time with her, he would soon be deeply committed to someone who could not share his deepest commitments to God, someone who could never fully understand who he, Peter Berkhardt, really was. All of Peter's life centered on his gratitude to Jesus Christ for offering his body and blood for forgiveness of sins and redemption to a life of fellowship with and service to God. He knew he could never share his life with someone who had not made that same commitment to God He also knew he could not maintain a casual friendship with Caroline. So, he did the only thing he could do. Peter committed Caroline into God's hands, asking his Heavenly Father for her to come to know Jesus Christ as her own Savior. He plunged into his work, resolving to avoid every opportunity of going home; and throwing himself on the mercy of God, he hoped that time and distance would resolve or heal his dilemma. He could see no other way, and as her presence continued to haunt him, he continued to pray faithfully for her salvation. It was not an easy course to follow, but it was his only option. She was so young, so vulnerable, so beautiful. He must give God opportunity to work out something that was beyond him.

Caroline's dinner party was a great success. She chose a snow-white tablecloth from the china cabinet drawer and set the table with classic Lenox china. The Waterford crystal and the sterling silver glimmered in candlelight. An enormous Peace rose from the yard floated in a cut glass bowl at the center of the table, drawing admiration for its creamy white base blushed with a hint of the colors of sunrise. She had filled lovely salt and pepper shakers, a delicate cream and sugar set, and a silver butter dish. Her homemade rolls with a hint of rosemary accompanied Caesar salad. For her main course she served tender eye of round roast, garlic mashed potatoes, and fresh green beans. She had learned through her various "families" how to cook a variety of foods and chose a menu she was certain these particular guests would enjoy. She knew what she liked and she knew how to prepare and season food well. She loved every minute of the preparation. She loved being able to shop and prepare the delicious dishes that seemed to appear effortlessly as the meal progressed. The Larsons and Lockwoods never guessed how much this first feast meant to her.

John Lockwood buttered his fourth roll and enjoyed the effect of real butter and the hint of rosemary in the bread, with a bite of roast. "Delicious, Miss Caroline!" he said with a twinkle in his eye.

"The meat's so tender, I know it's been cooking all day," added Martha.

"Think of the meals we've enjoyed around this table with Caroline's grandparents," said Millie Larson with a distant look in her eyes. "And here we are with Caroline. I just can't get over it. We feel so privileged to know you. It's just too bad your grandmother can't have the blessing of knowing you. She wanted that so badly."

Caroline didn't know what to say.

"Well, Dear," said Millie's husband Sam, whom Caroline knew only slightly. "God knows best. We get to enjoy this delightful young lady as an answer to her grandmother's prayers. We are blessed, Caroline!"

Throughout the evening she heard only generalities of Peter being back at school and hard at work. She resolved to put him from her mind as she herself would soon be hard at work with stakes which were high indeed. She must succeed and become self-sufficient or loose the life she had only just discovered.

After dinner, her adoptive grandfathers gallantly investigated the new furnace with her and made sure that it was operable. All of them laughed their way to the greenhouse to explain its marvels to Caroline once they had cleared and done the dishes. They didn't sit in the living room like proper company until Caroline, with the ladies' assistance, had served coffee and a very special chocolate fudge cake. They somehow managed to extract a promise from Caroline to ride to church with the Lockwoods on Sunday and were so gracious that they left her at the end of the evening feeling as though she had been the guest again instead of the hostess.

Caroline's church attendance became a regular occurrence, sometimes including outings with the college group and often including an invitation to dinner in a restaurant or in the Lockwood or Larson home. Even after school began, Caroline continued to enjoy her involvement with these people so much that she knew she would miss it if it discontinued. Occasionally she overheard someone mention Peter, but she was careful never to inquire after him. If he didn't need her, she didn't want anyone to think she needed him.

Caroline thoroughly enjoyed being a student at the university. Feeling somewhat secure for the first time in her life, she thrilled with the challenge, the discipline, and the adventure. She was doing something she loved, and something that took all of her best efforts, for she was determined to perform at the top of her class. As the weeks passed, she had the satisfaction of settling into a routine and seeing her plans succeed. Thanks to an anxious review of her budget on a regular basis, it began to look as though she could scrape by for the time being without selling any of Grandmother's valuables. Her journal readings continued to reveal both her family and the kind of family life she had never really experienced as an only child growing up in foster homes. She loved the discoveries of her grandmother's life and her mother's childhood and devoured her grandmother's accounts of purchasing and moving into the house they had ultimately left to Caroline.

I do love the house. It seems so extravagant, but Jack says it's just what we need. I would be happy with less if Jack could be here. Brad wants a

Caroline, deeply moved, wept, not unhappily, at
memories of a simple tea party that her own mother had
provided for her. She must have been very young at the time,
but she could still feel her own Teddie's soft plush fur and
satin ribbon, squeezed tightly in her arms. She could taste the
lemon squares her mother made for special occasions. She
even remembered the smell of the lemon juice when she had
helped her mother make them. Now she knew where those
memories had originated. How special it must have been to
her mother, Candice, to replicate her childhood memories for
her own daughter!

The next morning, Caroline found her grandmother's

recipe for lemon squares in a well-used state in one of several recipe boxes and added the ingredients to her shopping list. She tried to remember the times her mother had made lemon bars. It must have reminded her of home. But why hadn't Caroline known her grandparents? The drive to find out what had happened continued to draw Caroline back to the journals, but also filled her with dread.

Caroline continued to read the book of John every morning. She had decided to stick to the daily readings in the study guide because each day covered only a few verses. She had also begun to actually attempt to write answers to the questions in the guide, to write a quick summary of what happened in those verses, and then to also look for the principles behind what was said. It had taken her a while to realize that the focus of the study guide seemed to take her beyond the events to the reasons behind what was happening. The goal seemed to be to extract principles and truths about God that she could apply to her own life. She didn't understand everything, but using this process every day continued to reveal truths about Jesus that she had never known. Apparently, Jesus was willing to help with problems if she asked, if she was willing to do what he wanted. She wondered if it would be hard to do what he wanted. What would he want from her? The latter part of chapter two made her uncomfortable. Jesus knew he was going to die on a cross and be resurrected? He seemed to have a perspective that placed greater importance on these truths that seemed so ephemeral, than on the magnificent temple building everyone else thought was so important. Were there things that were more important for her than this brick and mortar house of her grandparents? She supposed it was true. Yes, the house had grounded her, but it was what the house represented that had given her the motivation and focus she had so badly needed. It was the unseen part of her heritage that she was still seeking. There was still a hole in her insides and there were still missing pieces to the puzzle of who she was.

ᦞ CHAPTER SIX ᦞ

Caroline's life was full of hard work, yet increasingly full of people who seemed to be continually caring for her. She had come to accept that God had actually heard and answered her prayer for people in her life who cared about her. She had to admit that she was glad she had allowed these people who called themselves her adoptive grandparents into her life. She actually enjoyed being with them. Still, it was with a secret hope to see Peter again that she accepted a Thanksgiving dinner invitation from his grandparents.

"One shouldn't be alone on Thanksgiving," she imagined him saying. She doubted that either the Larsons or the Lockwoods would allow her to be alone on such a day, and she was glad. She'd learned that Peter's family, as well as the Larsons, would be coming to the Lockwoods for dinner, so she tried to look forward to it without being nervous, and dressed carefully in her best autumn casual clothes. She loved the colors and comfort of her new brown boots with the pants, top, and cotton sweater. When her dinner rolls, a special request from Martha and John, had finished baking and were staying warm in a food carrier, she added a soft scarf of moss green around her neck and approved of what she saw in the mirror.

His car wasn't there yet when she walked next door, but she was introduced to his parents, Claire and Bret Berkhardt, and his sister, Jo. They welcomed her and seemed friendly and normal, though refined. It wasn't until the Larsons and many other guests had arrived, every chair was filled, and heads were bowed for prayers of thankfulness, that Caroline knew Peter wasn't coming. His mother and grandmother couldn't have known how much Caroline was in agreement with their lament at his absence. He had never missed a family holiday before, they said. His work must be very demanding, more demanding than they knew, as demanding as he had been insisting it was! How good that he had this wonderful opportunity for a doctorate but was almost finished! For some reason she didn't understand, Caroline felt guilty for sitting there at his grandparents' beautifully decorated Thanksgiving table, surrounded by his immediate and extended family, and the Larsons who had known him all his life. She felt part of the family, just like a cousin or sister she thought resignedly. A new member had joined his family and he didn't even know. It didn't seem right somehow.

"I'm sorry you can't be with your family today," commented Peter's real sister, Jo. Caroline had learned that she attended a Christian college on the other side of town,

88

when they were seated next to each other.

"I don't really have any family," Caroline admitted. "My parents both died when I was young." She tried to sound as matter of fact as she always did when discussing her parents.

"I'm so sorry. I guess I didn't know or had forgotten. Please forgive me."

"It's okay." Jo seemed genuinely sorry, so Caroline gave her the typical response that seemed to reassure people. "I grew up in good foster homes."

"I'm glad, but I don't suppose it's the same at all," Jo commented.

"No," Caroline acknowledged. "I'm really glad to be here in my grandparents' home so I can go to the university," she continued, eager to turn the conversation to less dangerous emotional ground.

"So, how are your classes going?" asked Jo.

"Great! How about you?"

"Well, I'm spending hours and hours on Greek, but enjoying every minute of it."

"The Greek language? Are you planning to live in Greece?" Caroline asked, surprised.

"No. I don't know yet where I'll live, but it's ancient Greek I'm studying. It's what the New Testament of the Bible was originally written in."

"I guess it wasn't written in English. But we have English Bibles. Aren't they good enough?"

"Yes, they are. They are all very good translations for different reasons. But anytime you translate something into another language you lose little nuances of meaning. I want to know every little nuance of the original writing so that I will be better able to explain it in another language, whatever language I have to learn where I end up living. I plan to be a missionary in another country. I want to be able to explain about Jesus to the people who live there the best that I can in their language."

"So, you'll have to study another language after you learn Greek?"

"Probably. I did study some French and a lot of Latin in high school, so I'm hoping it will help me a little, like it's helping a little now with Greek."

"Why do you want to be a missionary? How can you stand to leave your family?" Caroline asked, not realizing that her question revealed her own neediness.

"I want people to come to know Jesus, more than I want anything else in the world."

"Does Peter think like that?" Caroline couldn't help but ask.

"Yes, but I don't think he will be a missionary in another culture. Maybe, but he seems to think the Lord wants him to stay here and try to be salt and light. To try to be a positive influence on the business community. He's already led several classmates to the Lord."

"Oh."

The talk turned back to school and on to other topics, but Caroline turned this new information about being a Christian over and over in her mind as she enjoyed Grandmother Lockwood's moist roasted turkey, creamed corn, mashed potatoes, and perfect gravy. Peter's mother Claire had brought a sparkling mandarin orange salad, and Jo's tossed salad added freshness. Everyone was busy complimenting Martha on the turkey and her other specialties, along with everyone else who had contributed their own favorite wonderful dishes.

"It wouldn't be Thanksgiving without your homemade creamed corn, Grandma," said Jo as the bowl of milky white and golden goodness was passed around the table.

"I love the touch of rosemary in the rolls, Caroline," Peter's mother commented.

As the meal progressed, each person at the table shared what they were especially thankful for that year. When it was her turn, Caroline said that she was thankful for her new home and for her new adoptive grandparents, ending abruptly because she suddenly knew that if she said another word she would cry in front of all of these people and embarrass herself in a way she never had before. Martha graciously covered Caroline's embarrassment by saying how much they enjoyed their new neighbor and granddaughter.

"And now it's time for those amazing pies everyone has brought!" Martha continued.

"I'll have to have a small slice of pumpkin pie since it's Thanksgiving, but make sure I get some of Millie's amazing apple pie before it's gone!" requested her husband, Sam.

As they cleared the table later, Caroline managed to whisper, "Millie! That apple pie *was* amazing. It must be from scratch. I'd love to know how to do that! Is there any chance you could show me how to make it sometime?"

"Sure! I'll email the recipe and then come over sometime. You let me know when you want to make it," she whispered back.

Everyone was talking and laughing when Peter's phone call came. Various family members talked to him, but no one offered her the phone and of course he didn't ask to talk to her.

"He may not even know I'm here," she reminded herself. "Even if he did, I don't suppose I would have any right to expect to talk to him. He has his own life."

But after the phone call, his parents and grandparents mourned the fact that he was evidently "all grown up" and did have "his own life." Somehow, they had always thought Peter would settle close by and be part of their own community and lives. He had promised to come home for Christmas, and they would have to be content with that. Most likely he would meet someone, marry, and move away! After all, no one knew where he would find work in his field when he finished his doctorate. He was certainly old enough to make his own decisions. Grandmother Martha sent a silent prayer heavenward for God's will in Peter's life, which joined the prayers of other members of the family. She also sent up another secret prayer for Caroline's salvation, whether or not she was meant for Peter. She had made sure they met, but Grandmother Martha was certainly not going to interfere beyond that. God well knew the suffering caused by Caroline's grandmother marrying an unbeliever. It had taken God a good many years to set that right, and here was Emily's granddaughter, apparently still not safe in God's family.

Jo, astutely accepting that most young ladies who met her brother Peter quickly acquired the hope of meaning more to him than other young ladies, suddenly realized that Caroline had successfully hidden her feelings for Peter from the rest of the family and perhaps from Peter himself. From that moment on, she began to pray in earnest for Caroline's salvation.

Peter, for his part, was sitting alone in his apartment after coming home from Thanksgiving dinner with a friend's family. He could hardly stand not being home with his own family and thought himself foolish for staying away after he hung up. Perhaps Caroline wasn't even a part of their lives. Perhaps she would never become a Christian. Perhaps she had already accepted Jesus. Why hadn't he asked about her? Grandmother had merely written in passing that Caroline seemed to be enjoying her studies. Peter spent a considerable amount of time that night praying for God's will in her life and his own. No matter what the outcome between them, let her find her way to salvation in Christ, he prayed.

With so many prayers ascending for her salvation, Caroline went home and spent a very restless evening, went early to bed, couldn't sleep, and began reading her grandmother's journals again. It was a heartbreaking tale as Brad became hardened, began hanging out with the wrong crowd, and soon began to waste his life in their activities.

I know Brad is drinking heavily, just like Jack. Oh, God protect him from harm. Please, please don't let him hurt anyone. Please deliver him from alcohol. Deliver Jack. Protect Candice.

When Brad joined the marines upon graduation and she had to say goodbye, it was with a great deal of fear that his mother continued to pray for his well-being. Caroline's mother, Candice, began to follow similar patterns of behavior. Many nights Grandmother's journal was filled with desperate prayers on her behalf. When Candice eloped with an older man of loose reputation, Grandmother's heart broke with grief and anxiety. Caroline learned things about her father she had never known and didn't want to know. Her grandfather had forbidden her mother to date him or see him, with just cause, yet she had run away with him. Caroline finally fell asleep with her grandmother's most desperate plea to God swimming in front of her weary tear-filled eyes.

Please, God, whatever it takes, bring Brad and Candice into relationship with you. Save them from themselves, Jesus. Please, God, stop this evil that began with my disobedience. Break this cycle of evil holding my children from you and let the generations yet to be born walk with you. I can't bear it if my children and their families live in rebellion against you. Please forgive me and intervene in their lives and Jack's life. Please don't let my grandchildren fall prey to alcohol, this demon that rules Jack's life. Please deliver Brad from the drugs that are destroying him. I can't bear it! Jesus, please save them. Please let my children and their descendants walk with you. Deliver them from alcoholism and drug addiction. Let them know the joy of forgiveness, the joy of knowing Jesus. Whatever the cost. Whatever it takes. Jesus, I can't bear to see my future grandchildren suffer from these evils. Please break the chain of addiction now, before it's passed on to them. Let my grandchildren and all of my descendants serve you instead, Jesus.

Caroline woke with a heavy heart and a sense that there was something she must do. What was it that her grandmother had prayed? She pulled the open journal toward her and began to read. Her grandmother had prayed for them all to be delivered from alcohol. How strange that, in all of the foster homes she had seen, alcohol had never been abused! She had never been around it much. In fact, the smell was repulsive to her. As for drugs, she had decided to abide by elementary-school-aged promises to abstain and she had stuck with her decision because she had been so anxious to become independent and successful. To be delivered from addiction, no matter what the cost, had been her grandmother's prayer. What else had Grandmother prayed for her children and grandchildren? For her family to know Jesus, no matter what the cost! Her grandmother had prayed for her, Caroline, to know Jesus, before she had even existed. No matter the cost. What did that mean?

That night, Caroline read on through the months of not hearing from son or daughter, of finally hearing from Candice that she was married and that she would write again though she gave them no address or way to contact her. Caroline read through months of worried prayer for Brad in the thick of battle, and of the simple, chilling notice of his death. She read through her grandmother's anguished pleas for some assurance that he had turned to the Lord in his final moments. She read through her grandmother's doubts and self-recriminations connected with his death.

How could I have prayed such a prayer: no matter what the cost? God, surely you love him even more than I do. Why didn't you answer my prayers? Is this your answer, God? Will I ever see my son in heaven? Help me to understand, to trust that you were in this. Bring good out of this somehow, God. Only you can do that.

Caroline went through the motions of life each day, but her heart and mind were caught up in her grandmother's journal. She read morning and night, enduring her grandmother's grief. She too wondered where God was when her grandmother needed him. It was a full six months of journal entries later that her grandmother's doorbell had rung and a young soldier stood respectfully with hat in hand to tell her that he was a Christian who had stood next to her son when he'd been killed.

"I waited until I could tell you in person. Brad gave his life to Christ and was baptized by our chaplain the day before he died. When he was wounded, I stayed with him, praying. He knew he wasn't going to make it. He wanted you to know that he'd asked for God's forgiveness. He went smiling into the arms of Jesus. He made me promise to come and tell you that your prayers did not go unanswered, Ma'am. 'You have to thank her for her prayers,' he said. He said to tell you he knew how much you loved him. He made me promise to come and tell you."

Caroline's tears were added to the marks of her grandmother's tears on the journal page, which had fallen as Grandmother wrote simply, "Thank you, Jesus."

So Uncle Brad had given his life to Jesus in the end. God *had* heard Grandmother's prayers. But what of Caroline's own family, of Candice and her father, what of her own birth and childhood? And what now? What did all of this have to do with her?

Caroline got out of bed, showered, and ate a quick breakfast. She was afraid somehow to read her grandmother's Bible. Was her grandmother's God so powerful that he really could answer prayer? If God made the stars and sunsets, why hadn't she known her own grandmother? Why hadn't she known about this God? Had her mother known him before she died?

That night, Caroline settled in to read in a comfortable sofa in her grandmother's third story retreat. She was determined to find the answers. Her grandmother had left her this house and these journals so that she could.

Jack is desolated by Brad's death, but in denial about how it has hurt him. He has no trust in you, Lord, to ease the pain. He has no joy over Brad's

*salvation and no rest in knowing Brad is with you
now. Please bring him your peace, Lord. The alcohol
is worse, and he talks wildly about Candice and
Robert. I'm afraid of what he might do. He says he's
going to hire a private investigator to find them. Oh,
Father, I want to know where they are. I want my
daughter! But please don't let him find them if it will
only cause more harm.*

Grandmother was comforted by news from Candice that
they were expecting their first child and that Candice would
come soon for a visit. But it wasn't until Caroline was two
months old that she and Candice suddenly appeared. Only for
the day, Candice had insisted. Robert didn't know where she
was. He hadn't wanted her to have any contact with her
family, but she had to show them their granddaughter. How
her grandmother had rejoiced over and loved that little baby
Caroline! How she grieved when Candice left, not revealing
her location. How Emily had prayed for her daughter, son-in-
law, and granddaughter Caroline!

When the detective Jack secretly hired managed to locate
Candice after the visit, it had caused nothing but bad
feelings. They were now living only an hour away. In spite of
Robert's objections, Candice and Caroline came to visit more
and more frequently, but always in secret. Candice confided
her growing fear of her husband, Robert, his addiction to

alcohol, and her certainty that he wanted to take them away, out of reach of her parents. Emily had prayed earnestly, and Caroline read of many happy times she and her mother had spent with her grandmother. Here was her grandmother's love for Caroline and her mother poured out on the pages of her journal. Here was the proof that Caroline's memories of a loving, happy family were real. Robert was rarely present, but Grandfather Jack had relished the few times between business trips that he could spend with his daughter and granddaughter. Birthday and Christmas gifts, Easter baskets, and Thanksgiving dinners had all been part of Caroline's early childhood, but only intermittently.

I made Caroline a soft, white wool cape with a hood for her fourth birthday.

Caroline remembered that cape! How she had loved its warmth and softness! Her grandmother had made it for her! She hadn't known! What had happened to keep her forever separated from her grandparents?

❧ CHAPTER SEVEN ☙

School became increasingly difficult as the end of the semester loomed ahead. Caroline was caught up in trying to do her very best or better in each course. She loved what she was doing, but the projects would have been more enjoyable if there had not been so much to do. She ate, slept, and went to school. That was her life, but it was what she wanted.

As Christmas approached, Caroline tried not to think about her past Christmas experiences. They were anything but memorable. She had always received practical gifts, then sat by and watched the children of the house be showered with what they had especially requested and more. She had learned at a young age not to express interest in their gifts because it only led to jealousy, conflict, and rejection. Christmas was not something she looked forward to. She tried not to want to spend Christmas with the Lockwoods. It was one thing to invite a total stranger into your home for Thanksgiving, but an entirely different matter to invite someone for Christmas. What was Christmas like in their household? Peter had told them at Thanksgiving that he would come home, but she told herself she was really more interested in their family traditions. What would it be like to be part of such a family? How would she endure Christmas alone?

"It's better to be alone than to be somewhere I don't belong!" she told herself fiercely. She decided she would buy herself something special. Something small and inexpensive, but something she had always wanted. She would plan a special menu, and come up with Christmas activities like singing and playing carols on the piano and maybe watch a special Christmas movie. She would decorate the house! It didn't matter if no one else saw it. Maybe she would have someone over!

"There isn't anyone," she told herself.

Reading a few verses of John each day and answering the questions in the study guide showed the power of Jesus over and over. He healed the sick. He miraculously fed people but claimed to be a better, eternal food and drink himself. He could free people from sin. Jesus could heal her own hurts. What fear was keeping her from asking him to?

Thank you, Jesus! Candice prayed to ask you into her heart today, to come in and control her life. Thank you, Jesus, that she knows you now! Thank you for saving her, forgiving her, and making her a new person. Protect her from Robert and Jack's power struggle. Lord, she confessed how weak she is, how her addictions seem so powerful, how Robert has used her addictions to control her. Jesus, deliver her from that power. Hear her prayer to deliver her little daughter Caroline from such a heritage.

Caroline cried with shame and relief all at the same time. Her mother had believed in Jesus! That meant Candice was in heaven. Her grandmother's prayers had been answered! But her father and mother, the ones she loved best in all this world had not been parents to look up to. All of these years, all of her hopes to discover her heritage, all had been based on a silly little-girl understanding of life, she thought bitterly. All of her attempts to live up to the unreal image of them that she'd had in her mind mocked her now. How foolish she had been, to think that she was someone special, that she could make something special of her life!

Oh, God! How could you take Candice so soon? I still can't believe she's gone.

Caroline abruptly dried her eyes and continued reading the journal entry from the following day.

Jack is destroyed because he was at fault in the accident. The car was totaled. Forgive me God, but I'm

Finally, Caroline knew how her mother had really died. Her mother had died in a car accident and her grandfather had been driving! Had he been drunk? She pushed the journal away from her, deeply disturbed by what she had discovered. Could it get any worse than that? Sickened, she couldn't read any more.

School became more and more demanding for Caroline. It was just as well, because she had no desire to go back to reading her grandmother's journals. Although she held herself aloof from many of the activities of the college group, she thought some of them sounded fun. Maybe she would join in at some point. Once classes were ended for the term, it was going to be a long time until they started up again. In the meantime, she was consumed by finishing final projects and exams with as near perfection as she could manage. She didn't need to think about Christmas yet.

"Hey, Caroline!" said Jo the next Sunday when they both showed up for lunch at the Lockwoods' invitation. "I'll be driving right past your campus on my way to the mission Thursday night. We can always use more hands to help serve the meal. There are a lot of homeless people there! Can I pick you up about four?"

"Uh, sure," she replied, caught off guard. How could she

explain her reluctance when it came from too much personal familiarity with poverty and helplessness? She could easily be homeless herself right now if things had turned out differently! She would beg off later in the week.

"Great! We can talk about Christmas then."

"Sure," Caroline repeated, clueless.

"See you Thursday in front of the student center at four!" Jo said as she backed her car out of the Lockwoods' driveway.

Christmas? What about Christmas? Was there some other project Jo was working on?

"I guess helping some poor family celebrate Christmas is better than no Christmas at all," Caroline grudgingly admitted to herself. But if she didn't like it, she wasn't going to get roped into doing it! She had already agreed to pack food baskets for poor families on Saturday with the college group from the Lockwoods' church. She really couldn't give time to Peter's family's church as well. Wasn't going to one church enough?

On Thursday, she finished her last final exam and crossed the campus toward Stubin Student Center. She had worked hard, and she was tired but relieved to be done. She had been too busy studying to back out on tonight, and there was Jo's car, parked and idling, right in front.

"Hi!" smiled Jo, as Caroline swung her backpack in and climbed in after.

"Hi!"

"You look a little tired. It's going to be a while until we've served the dinner and get to sit down to eat what's left. Want to stop for a burger?"

"Sounds good," Caroline agreed, sinking into the warmth of Jo's car.

"Are you going anywhere for Christmas?" asked Jo.

"No," replied Caroline, surprised.

"Oh, I thought maybe you'd be going back to the town you came from."

"No, there really isn't anyone there that I'm related to."

"Oh. But I thought maybe one of the families you grew up with would want you to spend the time you have off with them."

"No. I wasn't really with any one family that long." That seemed the easiest way to explain that there was no one in any of those families with whom she would want to spend a single day. It was true, for the most part: she had never spent more than a couple of years with any one family. Even the last three years with Mr. and Mrs. Axel hadn't created a bond between them. Mr. Axel was always ill, and Mrs. Axel had very little energy and few interests. When her husband had died, she had merely sold everything as quickly as possible. It had hurt Caroline that, in spite of the faithful work she had done for them, Mrs. Axel had hardly thanked her and had seemed unaware of Caroline's needs. Caroline had received nothing, not even a keepsake from the garage sale she helped set up, except for a few things she had purchased.

"So how many classes and tests do you have left? Any papers to write? Software projects?" asked Jo.

"I'm finished!" acknowledge Caroline. "I just took my last test."

"Wow! I'm finished, too. Isn't it a great feeling?"

"I guess I've hardly had time to think about it," said Caroline, wishing she could just go home and be alone. She needed sleep.

Jo pulled into a fast-food drive.

"My treat!" she smiled.

Caroline was cold and tired, and the hamburger tasted great.

"They're expecting about a hundred for the meal tonight. There are six of us coming to serve. You know Julie from my grandparents' church, and there'll be three others from my church. There's a church service first. Kari and I are singing, and Matt is preaching. Then we serve the food and clean up. They use paper plates and cups, but it still takes a while to clean up. I really appreciate you coming."

"Sure," Caroline replied briefly, taking another bite of her burger.

"These people really need help. So many of them are addicted. Drugs. Alcohol. They really need Jesus. The mission was started years ago, jointly by our church and my grandparents' church. We try to do more for them through the winter months when the demand kind of drains their resources."

Caroline thought with shame of her own family. The family she had idealized. The family that she now knew had been ruled by drug and alcohol addiction. The family whose history she wanted no one to know. The heritage she had so eagerly sought, but wanted only to forget.

When they arrived, Caroline helped carry in several crockpots full of beef stew and thirty loaves of day old French bread. She met Matt, who was speaking that night, and the other helpers as they all bustled around the kitchen, prepping as much as possible before the church service. When it was time to begin, all of the volunteers were led up the center aisle and ushered to the platform. Caroline wanted to sink into the floor. There was no place she would have rather *not* been sitting than up there, pretending to be a Christian, pretending to care about these outcasts of society. She was only glad she wasn't sitting out there, one of them, but she knew she didn't belong on the platform with Jo, Matt, and the others. Caroline endured the welcome from the mission leaders, the song Jo and Kari sang, and Matt's cheerful greeting and prayer asking for God's blessing on their study of his Word tonight.

"I want to talk to you tonight about Jesus," Matt began. "In John chapter four, there is a true story from Jesus' life that tells us so much about God's love for us."

Caroline tried to remember John chapter four. She had skipped reading her grandmother's Bible a lot of mornings lately. She'd told herself she was too busy and too tired. Matt read several verses out loud to his audience before stopping to explain that most people would not go through the area known as Samaria in Jesus' day, even if it was the shortest route to their destination. In fact, most religious people went the long way around because they considered the people of Samaria socially and religiously unacceptable.

"This woman who came to get water from the well was used to rejection. Not only was she a Samaritan, she actually had ignored God all of her life. All her life, she had said no to God, and now she was reaping the consequences. She lived in sin, in a lifestyle that caused her to be rejected by everyone. She was even rejected by the other Samaritans! She came alone to the well, and she certainly didn't expect Jesus to speak to her. But Jesus, it tells us in God's Word, *had* to go through Samaria. Why did he have to go through Samaria? For only one reason: to bring the good news of forgiveness from sin to those who needed it most. If *you* are about to give up, if *you* feel hopeless and helpless, you are just like that Samaritan woman on that very day when Jesus went out of his way to offer her God's love. We've come here tonight to offer you God's love, because every one of us has been in the same place you are: without God, hopeless, and helpless."

Caroline looked out at the motley audience, wondering to herself whether any of them would believe Matt's statement.

"You see, in God's eyes, there is no difference between someone with a college degree or a good job, and someone living on the street with no way out. It says in another place in the Bible, in the book of Romans, chapter three, verse 23, that all of us have sinned, that all of us fall short of God's glory. According to the Bible, we are all just like that woman at the well who met Jesus that day. None of us deserve anything from God except condemnation and judgment and destruction. But there's good news! That's what Jesus came to tell that Samaritan woman. He said in verse 26 of John 4 that he was the Messiah, the one they were waiting for to explain everything to them. He explained to them the same thing he explained earlier to a wealthy, highly-educated, upper-class man named Nicodemus. He explained that none of us can claim to be good enough for God. No matter who we are, rich or poor, uneducated or a doctor of law or medicine or anything else. Whether we try to live a good life and do what's right, or we're living sinfully, so sinfully that even other sinners reject us, none of us has enough righteousness to count one little bit with God. But God loves us and he sent Jesus to tell us we need to do something about that. We are all condemned in God's eyes. We were all born into this world, where everyone is already set up because of their sins, to be condemned by God. But God loved the world. He loves us! So, he sent his Son, Jesus, to save the world from God's judgment and condemnation. He made a way for us to begin life with God, to be born into God's family, to begin to really live. All we have to do is believe in Jesus, the One God sent to take away our sins."

Caroline tried to wrap her brain around the idea that there was no difference in God's eyes between herself and the worst of the most addicted, the most likely to live a wasted, self-centered life.

"God loves them!" she thought, her eyes seeking out the dirtiest, wildest looking ones in the room. "Can he really change someone like that?" she wondered.

"So, stop thinking about how bad everyone else is," Matt intruded on Caroline's thoughts, bringing her up short. "And start thinking about how to make *yourself* right with God. I encourage you to come up here right now. There are people from the mission waiting right up here to pray with you and help you find forgiveness. Jesus can deliver you from any addiction, from any trouble, from any sin. Many of the people who work here in the mission were on the street just like you until Jesus delivered them."

As Matt prayed for Satan's power to be broken, several people made their way to the front. Many who came were weeping. Caroline struggled with what was happening. She wanted to have her sins forgiven. She wanted to pray. What should she say to God? She couldn't go down there with the homeless to be helped. She just couldn't! She clutched the seat of her chair, feeling desperate, until Matt's prayer was over. Jo and the others led the way off the platform and down a side aisle to the kitchen. Caroline was glad to have something to do so she didn't have to think. Somehow she made it through the serving of food, managed to eat only a couple of spoons of stew, and helped with the cleanup though she felt more and more exhausted as the time dragged on. Jo spoke excitedly about the salvation of several at the mission that night as she drove Caroline home. Caroline let her talk, making few comments. By the time she stumbled up the stairs that night she was so tired she could hardly finish her usual preparations for bed. When she woke the next morning, the room spun around her. She hadn't been this sick in a long time.

◖◗

Jo pulled into her grandparents' drive, parked, and ran up to the door. She loved eating Sunday lunch with them. She cherished spending time with her grandmother in the kitchen, a place where she had been loved and nurtured. Though her godly parents had indeed deeply loved and nurtured her, there was an extra-special bond between Jo and her grandmother. They had shared many happy times in this kitchen.

"Everyone should have the overflowing love of godly grandparents," she thought as her grandfather prayed for the meal. She listened with affection to the sound of his voice as he asked God to bless the food and those who had prepared it.

Her grandparents wanted an update on all of her activities and plans, and her wish list for Christmas. It wasn't until they were clearing the dishes from the table, that she began to describe the evening at the mission on Thursday, and the response to Matt's preaching.

"It was so evident that the Holy Spirit was working," Jo explained. "There were several people who prayed to receive Christ. I'm praying that they'll really be delivered from their past, and become missionaries right where they are. Caroline came, but I'm not sure what she thought of it."

"Speaking of Caroline," responded Martha, "Dr. Calton asked about her this morning. It turns out she's quite brilliant. Recipient of the Gordon Grant! She's working on some major senior project in her sophomore year *and* planning to graduate early."

"Really?"

"Has she ever said anything about it?"

"No. She is rather quiet, isn't she… Wasn't she in church this morning?"

"No. I called and left a message yesterday with an invitation to lunch, but I didn't hear anything back from her.

I haven't seen lights in the house. I guess maybe she's gone somewhere for Christmas."

"She said she was staying here. She doesn't seem to have ties to any of the foster families she grew up with."

"How sad! You know, her mother's only sibling died young. She doesn't have immediate family. I wonder if there is extended family anywhere. It would have to be on her father's side. Jack and Emily both outlived everyone in their own families. And their daughter, Caroline's mother. So sad."

"What happened? "

"I guess we never told you. Um… Caroline's mother, Candice, was killed in an automobile accident. Jack was driving. It really sent Jack over the edge for a while. It wasn't until he became a Christian that he had any peace. Caroline was quite young at the time. The father took her away and they never saw her again as far as I know. Based on what Caroline said, I guess he died too, but I'm not sure exactly when. It's kind of strange, isn't it? No one left in the family except Caroline."

"I'm going over to see if she's home," Jo said with a frown.

"Here, why don't you take the steak? And the salad left from lunch," Martha said as she handed the containers to Jo.

"Okay. I'll be back in a while." Jo crossed the street and rang the bell. Getting no response, she rang again, then knocked loudly. "Is she here, Lord? I'm not sure what to do."

After knocking for some time, she finally headed back to her grandparents' house. "She's not answering her door, Grandma."

"Well, let's put the steak and salad away. Maybe she went somewhere for the weekend."

"I don't think so. You know, she was awfully quiet Thursday night, maybe not feeling well. I don't know. I wonder if she was coming down with something! I'm a little worried about her."

Martha studied her granddaughter's troubled face.

"We have her house key, Dear. Why don't you take it over and check the house. If she's gone, just make sure you lock it up, and we'll put the key away. No harm done!"

Martha retrieved the key from its hiding place and Jo made her way across the street again. After getting no response to another ring of the doorbell, she inserted the key and cautiously opened the door. Grandma had said the security latch could be on from the inside if Caroline was there, but the door opened, so Jo leaned inside and called out, "Hello! Anybody home? Caroline?" Perhaps she had an overactive imagination and Caroline had gone somewhere for the weekend. Maybe she'd received an invitation for Christmas after all. "Help her to be safe, wherever she is, Lord," she prayed as she began to make the rounds of the first floor rooms.

"What a lovely home. It's somehow grander than

Grandma and Grandpa's ranch style," she thought appreciatively. "Beautiful but impersonal." She compared it to the image she had of her grandparents' spreading, comfortable home filled with family mementos and photos. Glancing into the kitchen, she briefly surveyed Caroline's spotlessly elegant but empty domain. "Grandma's kitchen is top of the line too, but so much more lived in," she thought to herself.

She started up the stairs, calling. "Caroline? It's Jo! Are you here?" Even though it was broad daylight, she wasn't feeling comfortable being there. "Lord, protect me!" she prayed. "Caroline?" she called again at the top of the stairs.

She heard a faint, "Jo!" from down the hall.

"Caroline?" Jo knocked on the door she thought was the right one, the only closed one.

She heard a weak, "Come in."

Caroline was obviously sick in bed. Really sick.

"Caroline, are you okay? What can I do for you?" she asked, sitting beside her and putting a hand on her forehead. "You have a fever."

"Water," was all Caroline could say.

Jo hurried down to the kitchen and brought back a tall glass of ice water. She helped Caroline sit up to drink it.

"So cold," Caroline said, shivering.

"It's the fever. Have you had any acetaminophen?"

"Last night."

"Here, take some more. Try to drink all of the water."

"Thank you," Caroline whispered after a long drink. She settled back and closed her eyes. "I prayed you'd come."

"I'm sorry it took us so long to realize you needed us."

"It's okay."

Jo gently straightened the covers and a few things on the nightstand. "I'm going to go tell Grandma and Grandpa that you're sick, and then I'll come right back, okay?"

She got a weak nod from Caroline.

"I think she's got the flu, Grandma," she explained from her grandparents' doorway. "I don't want to give it to you. Just hand me my purse, and I'll call you later."

"Don't you get the flu!" Grandpa John exclaimed.

"She prayed that I would come. She really needs some help, Grandpa."

"We'll be praying, Dear," Martha assured her as she handed over her purse. "Call us! Let your mother know where you are."

"I will. Thanks!"

"Just leave water. Don't get sick," Caroline managed to say when Jo reappeared.

"I'll stick around a while and see if you need me. Let's take your temperature. Do you have a thermometer?"

Caroline shook her head no. "Grandparents' room," she managed to say.

Jo went to look and eventually returned with a digital

thermometer. "101. No worries now, just go to sleep. You'd better drink some more water. I'll be right back."

Caroline managed to drink a little more of the water she brought back, and Jo watched until she was sure she was asleep.

"Well, Lord, what should I do now?" she asked silently.

"Pray for her salvation."

Jo was startled by the response. It had not been literally audible, but this was one time there was no doubt about what God had said. She had rarely heard from the Lord so directly. She began to pray that Caroline would get well quickly, and that she would be able to talk with her about her salvation. A call to a friend who was a physician's assistant reassured her that she was doing the right things for Caroline, and that it was safe for Caroline to remain at home if Jo stayed to make sure she got liquids and to see if the fever diminished by Monday. She called her parents and grandparents to tell them she was staying the night and asked them to pray, then tended to Caroline's needs until her mother came with an overnight bag for her.

"Are you sure you should stay, Dear?" asked her mother.

"I'm sure. There's plenty of room. I'll sleep in one of the other bedrooms. I've had my flu shot, so no worries."

"We'll be praying anyway."

"I know. Thanks, Mom."

By evening, it seemed that the fever had lessened at least

temporarily, and by Monday morning, her temperature was normal. Jo fixed an appetizing breakfast, but Caroline could eat only a few bites. The flu and fever had left her exhausted.

By lunchtime, Caroline was able to sit up and eat a small portion of the chicken soup Martha had brought over.

"Well, you'll soon be feeling better now that the fever's gone," Jo said with a smile.

"Thank you," Caroline breathed. She slept through the afternoon, but had no appetite for dinner that night. Jo set aside the tray of soft foods she had prepared.

"Caroline, I know you don't feel well right now. Maybe later, would you like to talk about spiritual things? Would you like to give your life to Jesus?"

"Now," Caroline whispered.

"Do you want to pray right now and ask him to come into your heart and life and to make you a new person?" Jo asked, kneeling beside the bed.

"Yes."

"Do you remember John 3:16? Matt quoted it Thursday night."

Caroline surprised her by quoting slowly but clearly, "For God so loved the world that he gave his one and only Son, that whoever believes in him shall not perish but have eternal life."

"Do you believe that Jesus is God's Son? That he died for you, in your place, to take your sins away?"

"Yes," Caroline nodded.

"Just say something like this: Dear God, I know I'm a sinner." Jo waited while Caroline repeated her words. "I believe you sent Jesus, your beloved Son… to die on the cross because of my sins… I'm sorry for the things I've done that are wrong… Please forgive all of my sins… I ask you, Jesus, to come into my heart… and by the power of the Holy Spirit to make me new, a new person alive to God… I accept your gift of forgiveness and life with you forever… Help me to live for you from now on… Help me to be obedient to your Word and to abide in you, Jesus… Help me to live a life worthy of a child of the King… Help me to be a blessing to others and to bear much fruit for God's kingdom… Thank you, Heavenly Father… In your son Jesus' name, Amen."

Caroline was very weak, but her eyes were alight with a smile that had the strength to turn up the corners of her mouth.

"Thank you, Jesus!" rejoiced Jo.

"Thank you!" Caroline said, her eyes closing again. "Thank you!" She turned on her side and slid into a peaceful, healing sleep.

Jo prayed silently over her for a while, praising God and asking God to protect and bless Caroline's life and future walk with the Lord.

❧ CHAPTER EIGHT ❧

Caroline slept for twelve hours and woke Tuesday morning feeling fairly normal. She was weak, but there was such joy inside her she felt as though she would burst. She looked at the morning light trying to find its way through and around her window shade. It was good to be alive, as though a song were singing over and over inside of her, "Thank you, Jesus! Thank you, Jesus!"

From her bed across the hall, Jo heard her singing and smiled. "Thank you, Jesus!" she echoed, reaching for her robe. She headed for the kitchen, suspecting that Caroline would need to eat soon.

"I smell breakfast!" Caroline said twenty minutes later as she walked into the kitchen.

"Hungry?"

"Starved!"

Jo laughed. "I thought you might be. How are you feeling?"

"I'm sure the fever's gone. I'm feeling so much better!

Tired, but good," she said, sinking into a kitchen chair. "Let's eat in the breakfast room. It's through here," she said, pointing with her head and starting to rise. "What can I carry?"

"Just stay where you are. I'll take care of it."

"I owe you, Jo."

"For what?"

"For everything. For coming to find me. For helping me pray. For staying to take care of me."

"Wouldn't have missed it for the world."

"How have you managed? I'm so sorry I couldn't be a better hostess to you."

"No worries. My mom brought an overnight bag by for me. They've all been praying for you."

Tears spilled from Caroline's eyes and ran down her face, her typical stoicism overcome by physical weakness and by God's overwhelming kindness.

"Thank you."

"Caroline, everyone will be so excited to hear how God answered their prayers for your salvation."

"I can't wait to tell them!"

"Come on, let's eat! I think you need some food!" Jo scurried back and forth, getting them settled in the breakfast room with scrambled eggs, juice, and toast. "Why don't you pray and thank God for our food. And for anything else you want."

Caroline began hesitantly. "Dear God… you know how badly I needed you. Thank you for sending Jo and her grandparents, and all the others, to help me and to pray for me. Thank you for my grandmother's prayers. Thank you for answering her prayers. Thank you for protecting me all of the years I didn't know you. Thank you for this house. Thank you for sending Jo to help me when I was sick. Thank you for changing me and letting me be part of your family. Thank you for Jesus, and for this food. In Jesus' name, Amen."

"Amen!" They dived into breakfast while Jo silently talked with God about Caroline's salvation. "Who would you like to tell first about being born again?" she asked, knowing how important this was to Caroline's spiritual well-being and growth.

"Born again. Yes, that's what Jesus said to Nicodemus That's what happened to me."

"How did you come to know you needed Jesus?" she asked Caroline, truly curious.

"It was what I learned from reading the Gospel of John. Grandmother's Bible study of John. See? Right here. I started reading it when I first came here. It made me think about who Jesus really is. According to the disciple John, who wrote this book of the Bible, Jesus is God, Jesus is the only Son of God. He's the Messiah, the one people had been writing about and looking for, just like other, older books of the Bible talked about years before he was born. Like Daniel wrote about the Messiah looking like a human being, but one who was given authority and power over all people forever by God. I really didn't know all this about Jesus. It was so exciting to find out! And my grandmother's journals! She wrote about how God answered her prayers and saved her children. It was sad. I mean they died young, but she was just happy that they had accepted Jesus. I guess she prayed for me, too, for me to be saved. And the mission, the people at the mission."

"You mean Matt's message Thursday night?"

"No. Yes, but realizing I wasn't any better than those homeless, addicted people." Caroline stopped.

"I don't understand."

"I was angry at God all my life. I was angry at my parents and grandparents. I couldn't understand why they had all died and I'd had to grow up in foster homes. And then I found out my grandparents had been alive and I'd still grown up in foster homes! I just couldn't understand it. I was determined to find the heritage I thought I deserved, but I found a better one, a different one. My real heritage was worse, much worse in some ways. My closest relatives were all alcoholics and drug addicts. Not what I'd expected to find at all! But Grandma wasn't! She prayed for all of us, and God answered her prayers. It's funny, though. I thought it was so wrong to grow up in foster homes, all alone, but that's how God answered Grandma's prayers. That's how God protected me from addiction. He was protecting me from my own family! Grandma prayed for that, no matter what, she said. Now I understand."

"Wow!" was all Jo could manage.

"I don't know all of the story yet, but I know it was God. I believe that now."

"Wow."

"I want people to know that I'm a Christian now. But all of that about my family still seems kind of private. Do you mind not telling anyone? I don't know. Maybe everybody already knew all of that. Everybody but me," Caroline smiled a little ruefully.

"I didn't know. I don't know how much my grandparents knew."

"Maybe they still know more than I do. I haven't finished reading my grandmother's journals yet."

"I don't know. I won't tell anyone. It's up to you how much of your family's history you want to tell. But it might do other people good to hear how God worked. I mean his ways might seem harsh or wrong when we can't see the end, but look what he's done for you!"

Caroline began to weep again. "It still hurts. I wish it hadn't been this way."

"Of course not! I'm sorry!"

"No. No. It's okay. I'm so amazed that God would give me all of this, that he would do all of this for me. That he would give me salvation when I was angry with him."

"God is good."

"Yes. God is good."

"Do you know the verse that tells us Christ died for us while we were still sinners?" asked Jo. "This would be a good one for you to memorize. Here it is. Romans 5:8. 'But God demonstrates his own love for us in this: While we were still sinners, Christ died for us.' You know, some days we think we deserve the best. Other days, we feel so unworthy we think we don't even deserve the *gift* of God's salvation. Our thoughts and emotions are not really dependable. It's really important for you to spend time reading the Bible and talking and listening to God. Each day, as much as we can, we need to fill our minds with God's truth instead of our own feelings and thoughts. We even have an enemy, Satan, Christ's enemy, who will try to convince you that God's salvation isn't real. I want you to write down these verses and read them whenever you need to be reassured that your sins are forgiven and that you belong to Jesus now. Romans 8:38-39 says that no one, nothing, can separate us from God's love in Christ Jesus our Lord."

They found a place inside the cover of Caroline's grandmother's Bible and recorded Caroline's salvation with yesterday's date. Jo continued giving Caroline verses to write underneath. "Remember, you are part of your family, the family you were born to, no matter what they did or you do.

Now, you're also part of God's family, and nothing you or anyone else does can change that. God has adopted you and given you a new birth. It can't be undone. It's forever because God promised. You belong to him now. Here, let's look at I Corinthians 6:19-20. It says you are not your own because you were bought by God with the blood of Christ. He put his Holy Spirit inside you. Look at Ephesians 1:13-14 and 4:30. It says God's Spirit in us is like a guarantee. God's seal for the day of our redemption. He will never leave you, Caroline."

"Wow! It's like all the things I was looking for in a family, I have now."

"Yes! Only better! Eternal, unending, without limit!"

Caroline's face glowed with the realization of what believing in Christ meant.

"Who do you want to tell first?" Jo asked.

"Your grandparents. I want them to know. They've told me how Grandmother prayed for me. I want them to know God answered all of her prayers."

Jo picked up her phone. "I'm calling them right now."

"Now?" Caroline laughed.

"Now. Hi, Grandma! Caroline's feeling better. She'd like to talk to you." She handed Caroline the phone.

"Hi, uh, Martha! I want you to know I've given my life to Jesus. I wanted you to know that God answered my grandparents' prayers for me."

"Oh, Caroline. I'm thrilled! We've been praying for you too. Here let me put John on. He'd just love to hear your news!"

"Caroline?" she heard Jo's grandfather say.

"Yes! I called to thank you for praying for me. I've asked Jesus into my heart. I belong to him now."

"Caroline, I couldn't be happier if you were my own granddaughter telling me such great news!"

"Thank you. Thank you for all you've done for me."

"What have we done for you? Here, I'll put Martha on again."

"Caroline, how are you feeling?" Martha asked.

"I'm over the worst. Just weak. Jo's been taking good care of me."

"Are you ready to come over for lunch today? Or would tomorrow be better?"

"Maybe tomorrow."

"All right. Tell Jo to bring you over tomorrow."

"Okay. Thanks, Martha."

"Oh, just call me Grandma. And you'd better tell your other grandparents, Sam and Millie. They'll be so excited!"

"Okay," Caroline laughed. "See you tomorrow."

She told Jo what Martha had said about lunch and about calling the Larsons.

"Let's see, I think I have them here. Let's give them a call," Jo said, finding them in her phone directory. "Here you go."

"Hello, Millie? This is Caroline Engbert."

"Caroline! You must be feeling better. We heard you were sick."

"Yes, I'm feeling much better. But I called to tell you my news. I gave my life to Jesus yesterday. I wanted you to know."

Millie's voice broke with emotion. Caroline could tell she was crying. "Caroline, I'm so happy to hear you say that I've been praying! So has Sam! We've been so worried about you!"

Caroline was moved by Millie's tears. "Will you tell Sam?"

"Yes. He's not home right now. I'll tell him when he gets back. Is there anything you need, Caroline?"

"No. I'm just fine. I just need to take it slow and get my strength back."

"We'll be praying for a rapid recovery."

"Thank you! I'll catch you later, Sunday for sure if not sooner."

"God bless you, Caroline. I'm going to ask God to tell your grandparents! There'll be partying in heaven tonight!"

"Yes! Thank you, Millie. Goodbye!"

Caroline laughed as she told Jo about the party in heaven.

"It's true, you know," Jo responded. "Luke Chapter 15. Here it is. The first seven verses are a parable Jesus told to illustrate the truth in verse seven. Every time a sinner repents, there is great rejoicing in heaven!"

"I see," Caroline said. "They've probably been at it since yesterday!"

Jo laughed. "Probably! But you must be tired. How about you go lie down while I clean up. Then I should head for home and give you some peace and quiet until tomorrow."

"Thank you, Jo. I think I will lie down for a while."

"There's tuna all mixed in the fridge for your lunch. I'll go ahead and make the sandwich and leave it wrapped for you. All right if I put a petite sirloin and some cream of mushroom soup in the crockpot for your dinner? I saw the steaks in your freezer. Do you mind?"

"I don't mind, but you don't have to do that. I can find something to eat later."

"It won't take me long. You go lie down, and I'll just let myself out when I'm done. I'll see you tomorrow!"

"Thanks, Jo." Caroline didn't argue. She was too tired.

Later, when she woke, Jo was gone, but she could smell the beef in the crockpot. Even half-cooked it smelled amazing. It made her mouth water, so she went looking for the tuna sandwich. There was a tray with dishes and silverware on the kitchen counter. Jo had left potato chips on the plate, and a glass for water on the tray. In the refrigerator, Caroline found a wrapped sandwich and a plastic baggie of rinsed, peeled mini carrots. She took the tray all the way up to her grandmother's third floor study, picking up her grandmother's journal where she had left off.

Robert took Caroline today. He and Jack had fierce words after the accident. He's punishing Jack by taking Caroline away. He says he's leaving and we'll never find them. Oh, God, keep them safe. Grant that Caroline may somehow grow up free of this horrible legacy, free of addictions. Let her childhood be free from knowing this heritage we have left her. Keep her safe, Lord!

Caroline read on. Two months later, her grandmother discovered that Jack had filed for legal custody of Caroline. Six months later, her grandparents knew that would never happen: Robert's response, with the support of the courts, was a restraining order against her grandparents.

If I never see her again, please God, grant that she may somehow come to know Christ as her savior. Oh, God, keep Caroline safe. Someday, help her to know we love her.

Caroline knew from legal records she had seen and the date of the last entry in her grandmother's journal that her father had died soon after, rather suddenly. Evidently the state where they lived had no record of her grandparents.

Either that or the restraining order had influenced the decision to place her in foster care. She had grown up free of all that had happened, in answer to her grandmother's prayers. Still, it seemed strange that her grandparents had never attempted to contact her. The rest of the journal was blank, but there was an envelope taped to the back cover. Her name was penned across the front in her grandmother's hand. The letter inside was dated shortly before her grandmother's death.

Dear Caroline,

I hope someday that you will know how much your grandfather and I loved you. Please forgive us for any harm we have done you. We pray that you have grown up safely and happily. No doubt your father remarried and your stepmother has been a real mother to you.

Our attempts to contact you and your father have never been successful. If you have read this journal, you know we truly love you and hope that you will someday give your life to Jesus Christ. It wasn't until much later that Jack, your grandfather, gave his life to Christ. Perhaps it was for the best that his attempts to find you earlier were thwarted, but he was like a different person at the end. Jesus delivered him from his life-long addiction to alcohol, a true miracle. Oh how we longed to do something to show you how much you were loved!

I am old and ill now. All I can do is to leave you our home, and these journals to read. I pray that they will bring you peace and salvation rather than further harm.

I don't know how good can come of all this, but I leave it in God's hands. His ways are perfect. God bless you and keep you. I hope to see you someday in heaven.

With all my heart,
Your Grandmother Emily

Caroline's tears fell freely. If only she could have known them! But God had done what was best. Someday, she would explain to them, someday she would see them in heaven. She was sure of that now. Her grandparents had never known of her father's death! What strange disconnects! Yet all of it was God's doing, to bring her here to find her real heritage of faith in Christ.

"Thank you, Jesus! Thank you, Jesus!"

⚜ EPILOG ⚜

"Hi, Caroline. I called to let you know that my grandparents had to go help Grandma Martha's sister for a week or so. She fell and sprained her ankle, so they went to stay and help. Grandma asked me to reschedule our lunch for the end of next week."

"Hi, Jo. Your grandmother doesn't have to give me lunch."

"I know, but Grandma insists they'll be back by the middle of next week. She wants us to put a week from Friday on our calendars for lunch. And for decorating Christmas cookies!"

"Well, I could hardly turn that down!"

"Great! So anyway, can you come to *my* house for lunch tomorrow?"

"I don't know. I'm pretty much recovered. Just dragging a little."

"Not having a relapse, I hope."

"No. Not a relapse. I'm just tired."

"Well, Mom will fix us lunch if we'll help her decorate the house. You don't have to do that much. I'll do all the work and you can tell me what to do! We'll just do the inside. Dad does the outside lights. But, I need to pick up evergreen wreaths for the front door tomorrow. Can I pick you up after that? I have to put a wreath on Grandma and Grandpa's front door for them. Maybe around nine o'clock?"

"Okay."

"Do you need to go to the doctor? I could take you."

"No. I'm fine."

"Really?"

"Really. Sounds like fun."

"Well, if you're not feeling better by tomorrow, we can check in with a doctor."

"Okay. I'm fine."

Caroline was feeling more like her normally healthy self by the next morning, and she was looking forward to getting out of the house. It would be nice to do something different. She was curious, too, about Jo and Peter's family and home.

"I'm here," texted Jo the next morning. "Come on over to Gr & Gr's."

Caroline grabbed her coat, hat, and gloves and headed next door. Jo's car was parked in the drive, and she was busy unwrapping a wreath with a green scent so fresh they could have been in the snowy woods cutting it down right that moment. Caroline helped her carry it to the door and hang it

136

on the slender nail that was waiting.

"Nice!" exclaimed Caroline.

"I have to get the bow Mom sent along," explained Jo, dashing back to the car. "You'll have to help me fasten it on."

They decided the top center seemed the best location, managed to fasten it securely, and then stood back to admire the bow's long ribbon streamers stirring gently in the breeze.

"It does help the house look lived in. Okay, now I need to water Grandma's plants."

They made short work of Jo's duties inside and were soon on the road, the wreath for Jo's house infusing the car with its strong woodsy fragrance. Several matching swags and garlands contributed to the intensity of the aroma.

"I think Mom wants us to use them on the mantels and stairs. She ordered more than usual this year. The youth group at church sold them as a fund raiser. I'm going to need your help to come up with a sort of unifying look to tie it all together. We have a lot of decorations, but it's kind of a hodgepodge. Maybe you can help me choose what to use. By the way, can you come for Christmas dinner?"

"I... yeah, I would like that."

"Good. Thanksgiving is always at Grandma and Grandpa Lockwood's, but Christmas is always at our house."

"Okay."

As Jo drove, Caroline checked her own Pinterest pins for Christmas decorating and went on to search for other ideas. A lot would depend on the style of Jo's parents' home, but she showed some especially nice looks to Jo and got positive responses from her. They both began to be excited about the possibilities. Caroline was surprised at the modest home when Jo pulled up to the curb. It was a typical suburban neighborhood, with large two-story houses, but somehow Caroline had expected something different. As they began to unload greenery, Jo's mother came to help. Her welcome immediately relieved Caroline's anxiety.

"Please call me Claire. Jo tells me you're a new believer."

"Yes. Thanks to Jo!"

"I'm glad my daughter was helpful, but Jesus always gets the credit. I'm sure he was working in your life in other ways as well as through Jo. Isn't it wonderful that he loves us enough to pursue us?"

"Yes. That's true." smiled Caroline.

"Did you get Grandma's wreath up?" Claire asked, turning to Jo.

"Yeah, we did. The bow was perfect."

"I've set up the laundry room as your craft center, so I'll let you girls do what you want with the supplies we have. Thanks for coming to help, Caroline. Please excuse me: I have a Bible study to prepare, but I'll see you at lunchtime."

Jo pointed to the boxes in the living room. "Those are the decorations we have. We'll do the tree later, so we didn't bring those ornaments up yet. Let's go see what kind of other stuff Mom bought for us." Caroline followed her through the immaculate craftsman style home, trying with little success to ignore the many family photos that showed Peter at a variety of ages. With an effort at refocusing on the job at hand, she returned to analyzing the style and décor of the house. It was open, spacious, and so bright and airy that it appeared to be new.

"How long have you lived here?" she asked Jo.

"All my life."

"It looks like a new house."

"We just painted the whole first floor."

"That explains why it feels so fresh. I think my house could use a little fresh paint."

"Oh? Let me know. I'll help!"

"Really?"

"Sure. We probably don't have time to paint the whole first floor!"

"No. There's one room I'd really like to paint. The small one by the back door. The mud room. I call it the flower room because Grandma kept all of her vases and flower arranging supplies there. I'd like it to be fresh and bright. I haven't figured out what to do to make it look more like a place to arrange flowers, so let me know if you have any ideas."

"Artwork maybe? Or putting the vases on display?"

"Good idea! I'll have to think about it."

They discussed the ribbon, pine cones, and other accents Jo's mom had purchased or pulled out of storage; and Jo gave Caroline a tour, describing things they had done in previous years. After a review of their favorite examples from online, they decided on silver and white with the living green and just a few of the deepest red accents. They sprayed a dusting of silver paint on the pinecones and then began putting the green garlands in place while the pinecones dried. The oversized woodwork of the house created the perfect backdrop. Caroline wove a wide, silver-wired ribbon through each of the garlands and swags, as well as the wreath for the door. They attached the pine cones and shiny silver balls in a variety of sizes, and stood back to evaluate the effect. Caroline wasn't satisfied.

"Here. Look at this picture. We need more greenery with a different texture or a slightly different shade of green to really make it look lush. What evergreens do you have out in your yard?"

"Blue spruce trees. Pine trees. Pfitzers. Oh, the holly bush! We always put some holly somewhere."

"Great! Let's go!"

Jo got them each a couple of bags and a pair of pruning shears. They had a highly successful time combing the yard for useable greens and came in laughing and refreshed from the brisk work.

When they'd finally tucked their cuttings into the existing

arrangements, they were pleased with the added fullness, new textures, and more complex range of greens. The English holly added its distinctive shapes, and its deepest green along with the bright red berries. They searched out clear glass bases for each of the white pillar candles Claire had purchased, and then tied dark red velvet ribbon around the white candles. The result was stunning, but Caroline pointed out they were going to run out of candles if they continued to cluster them on each surface.

"The mantels really need larger candles at the focal point, too."

"Mom?" called Jo. "We're going to the store for more candles!"

"Okay! Let me know when you get hungry."

"It shouldn't take us long. See you later!"

Jo and Caroline found the oversized candles they were looking for and walked through the floral department on the way to the cashier. Caroline spotted sparkling sprays of miniature glass and silver jingle bells on sale. They were tiny, yet exquisitely done and would add just the right touch to finish off their decorating. Once they were home, it didn't take long to add the final details and start cleaning up.

"Mom! We're done! Come and see!"

"Oh, my!" exclaimed Claire, coming down the stairs. "It's beautiful! I'm afraid you're going to be stuck with this job every year! It's lovely!"

"Yay!" crowed Jo. "It was all Caroline's good taste!"

"No!" Caroline denied, turning pink with embarrassment.

"Yes!" insisted Jo.

"You did a wonderful job! The quiche is ready. Let's have some lunch."

"Okay, Mom. We just have a little more cleanup to do and then we can help."

The quiche was perfectly done and served with fresh pears and a tossed salad. Her illness followed by the morning's activities brought Caroline to the realization that she was hungrier than she'd thought. Jo thanked God for the food and asked him to bless it. She also thanked God for Caroline and her help that morning.

"Are you ready for your Bible study, Mom?" asked Jo as they began to eat.

"Pretty much. Just a few loose ends to tie up."

"Mom teaches a ladies' Bible study at our church each week. She's done it ever since I can remember," Jo explained to Caroline.

"Oh dear! Has it been that long? Maybe I should let someone else have a go at it."

"Come on, Mom. You know they appreciate your teaching or they wouldn't ask you to do it every year, and the ladies wouldn't keep coming."

"Well I hope I haven't gotten stale. Caroline, are you involved in a Bible study?" Claire asked.

"I'm doing a study of the Gospel of John,"

"Wonderful!"

"It's a study her grandmother had," Jo explained. "It's part of how Caroline came to the Lord. Like you said earlier, God was working in Caroline's life in so many ways. It's amazing!"

"How else was he working?" Claire asked Caroline.

"Well… I was reading my grandmother's journals and found out she'd been praying for me, even though we were apart. I can really see how God answered her prayers. There were lots of other things, too. Inheriting my grandmother's house and finding her journals still seems like such a miracle to me. Coming here and being able to go to the university. Dr. Calton's calendar."

"His calendar?" asked Jo.

Caroline laughed. "Yes! In his office the first time I met him. It had a verse from John that I'd just read that morning! I wasn't sure there was a God big enough and good enough to create the world, or to create the beauty of a sunset. I struggled with God orchestrating the sunset but doing such a bad job of orchestrating my life. It turns out he knew what he was doing." She didn't want to divulge the angry prayer for people to care for her, one more sign of God revealing his goodness to her. This mother and daughter were examples of how he had answered that prayer. "I guess God sent a lot of people, like the Lockwoods and all of you to help me believe him."

"That's wonderful, Caroline!" exclaimed Claire. "Are you doing your study of John with a group?"

"No. I'm on my own."

"It might be a good idea to join a group, too. It helps to hear other people's perspectives and it helps to be accountable to keep going, to keep doing the lessons."

"I don't know if I have time to do that during the school year."

"I know what you mean," agreed Jo.

"I guess you're not really involved in a group study right now, are you Jo?" asked her mother.

"It is hard with school and other commitments. I spend time with the Lord every day on my own. I would never give up that devotional time, but I'm not sure I can handle a group Bible study right now either." Jo turned to Caroline. "You do the study of John each day as a devotional, right Caroline?"

"Right. I guess so. I'm finding so much to learn from it every morning. It's so amazing!"

"Maybe I could get the same study, and we could do it separately but discuss it each week. We could text or FaceTime at least."

"That would be good! There are so many things I would like to understand, but there isn't anyone to ask."

"I think that's a wonderful idea!" exclaimed Claire.

After lunch, Jo ordered a copy of the same study of John. Caroline was amazed to see the number of studies on John that were available.

"John's a great book to study, and there are a lot of really good study guides," explained Jo. "John happens to be a great choice to learn about Jesus. God really has been working in your life, hasn't he? I realize every once in a while how oblivious I am to his work in my own life. I mean, he guides us, and protects us, and probably does so many kind things for us every day. It's easy to forget to stop and think about it and acknowledge his goodness in our lives."

"I was oblivious. I didn't know. I guess I'm so much more aware of that now. I have so much to be thankful for. I thank him every day!"

"I think that's what he wants us to do. Since he's the source of all good, that's where the good in this world comes from. All the good in our lives, too. All we have to do is thank him."

"So what can I bring for Christmas dinner? How many people will there be?"

"Let's see, our family, four. You, five. Grandma and Grandpa, seven. Grandma's sister makes eight. My mom's brother and his family, four more. You met them at Thanksgiving. That's twelve. We might make it around one table, but there could be more. We usually set up another table. I'll talk to Mom and see if there's anything she wants you to bring. I'll let you know the final count."

"I should probably go home. Would it work with your

schedule to take me back pretty soon?"

"Sure. We can go now. I think you might need a nap."

"I'm feeling great, but I am glad it's Christmas break. I needed a break."

"Me too! Let me know if you need a ride anywhere. If you want to go Christmas shopping, that would be fun. There are still a couple of great concerts coming up before Christmas, too."

They discussed some possibilities and then Jo dropped Caroline at her door. Caroline needed to think about Christmas. Buying Christmas presents seemed a difficult course to maneuver. She hadn't known how to talk to Jo about it. She wouldn't be expected to give to all of the people coming to the Berkhardts' Christmas dinner, but she would have to bring a hostess gift that would somehow contribute to the general celebration. She wanted to thank the Berkhardts and Lockwoods, and especially Jo. Should she get a gift for Peter? It would take some thought. It was not likely that he would give her a gift. She wanted him to know that she had given her life to Jesus. It seemed important. Maybe she should pray about it. It was comforting to know that Jesus really cared about her. She wondered how long Peter would be home. Just a day or two? Would she be able to get to know him better with all of those people around on Christmas day? She found herself hoping that he would want to spend some time with her but pulled her thoughts up short

146

when her mind began to invent reasons for him to come over and check out her tech center. Everything was working fine, especially since she'd had all of this down time after being sick. She'd spent a lot of time updating and eliminating any software glitches and conflicts. If only life were as simple. One thing was certain: this Christmas would be much better than all but her vaguest Christmas memories from long ago. Would it be awkward to be at the Berkhardts' celebration? She wished she knew if Peter had any thoughts about her. She refused to let herself think about how much she looked forward to seeing him. Was he always as much fun to be with as that Saturday they had spent together?

For More Information

For more information including a downloadable copy of the book of John devotional and updates about upcoming books, visit:

gailethulson.com

About the Author

Gaile Thulson holds an undergraduate degree from Wheaton College with double majors in Elementary Education and Biblical Archaeology, as well as a master's degree in Old Testament from Denver Seminary and two Master of Education degrees from the University of Northern Colorado. She loves learning and has enjoyed teaching a variety of subjects to a variety of ages in a variety of settings. Reading fiction is one of her favorite pastimes and, as a writer, she loves expressing her faith in Christ through the fiction genre, as well as nonfiction and poetry. Grateful for their spiritual heritage, she and her husband Mark enjoy passing the Christian values of their parents down to their own children and grandchildren.

Cup of Water Publishing

Giving a thirsty person a cup of water brings refreshment and can be lifesaving. Christ declared that such an action by his disciples would not go unrewarded. In the same way, giving a cup of spiritual water brings refreshment and can also be lifesaving. It is the mission of Cup of Water Publishing to give spiritual refreshment to any who are "thirsty" by making available material that is wholesome, Biblical, theologically sound, and edifying. Ultimately, our goal is to point the way to Jesus, the source of true spiritual water.